#7

Daredevil Over Niagara

THE MITCHELL 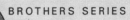 BROTHERS SERIES

#7
Daredevil Over Niagara

THE MITCHELL · BROTHERS SERIES

Brian McFarlane

Fenn Publishing Company Ltd.
Bolton, Canada

DAREDEVIL OVER NIAGARA
BOOK SEVEN IN THE MITCHELL BROTHERS SERIES
A Fenn Publishing Book / May 2005

All rights reserved

The content, opinion and subject matter contained herein is the written
expression of the author and does not reflect the opinion or ideology of the
publisher, or that of the publisher's representatives.

Fenn Publishing Company Ltd.
Bolton, Ontario, Canada

Distributed in Canada by H.B. Fenn and Company Ltd.
Bolton, Ontario, Canada, L7E 1W2
www.hbfenn.com

Library and Archives Canada Cataloguing in Publication

McFarlane, Brian, 1931-
        Daredevil over Niagara / Brian McFarlane.

(Mitchell Brothers series ; 7)
For ages 8–12.
ISBN 1-55168-275-3

        I. Title. II. Series: McFarlane, Brian, 1931- Mitchell
Brothers series ; 7.

PS8575.F37D37 2005   jC813'.54   C2005-903096-8

DAREDEVIL OVER NIAGARA

NOTE FROM THE AUTHOR

In the summer of 1860, Willie Hunt, a young Canadian from Port Hope, Ontario, journeyed to Niagara Falls where he performed incredible deeds high on a tightrope over the gorge linking Canada with the United States. Willie Hunt would soon become known as The Great Farini. It is breathtaking to envision Farini and his arch rival Blondin, the famous Frenchman, duelling for attention—and a sizeable fortune—high above the gorge, risking their lives with every bold step they took along their swaying ropes.

One day your author travelled to Niagara Falls, New York, and stood at Prospect Point overlooking the American Falls. I marvelled to think that Farini once mounted a pair of slender metal stilts and waded into the swirling waters above the very brink of the cataract, only to...but wait, I'm getting ahead of my story.

The adventures and deeds of Farini in the pages ahead are, for the most part, factual. The Mitchell brothers' trip down the River of Time to Niagara Falls, where they met this amazing man and witnessed his death-defying stunts, is entirely fictional.

The Great Farini rates a very special niche in Canadian history. Noted historian Pierre Berton called Farini "one of Canada's greatest unsung heroes." What Farini said at the time, how he felt and how he acted can only be imagined. That's why we call what follows "a story based on truth." I hope you enjoy it.

Speaking as a parent and grandparent, I caution my young readers never to attempt any dangerous ropewalking stunts as described in the pages ahead.

Brian McFarlane

CHAPTER 1

DAREDEVIL ON A ROPE

"I can't believe you are up there doing that," Marty Mitchell said, his head tilted upward, his eyes shaded with one hand. "I think you're crazy. It's the worst idea you ever had." Marty was watching his brother Max as he got ready to walk a thick strand of rope from one side of the barn to the other.

Max Mitchell was 17, broad-shouldered with a mop of unruly blond hair. He laughed and said, "You never know what you can do until you try. The rope is thick and I've always had good balance. And heights have never scared me."

"Well, they scare me," said 15-year-old Marty. His reddish brown hair stuck out from under his Yankees baseball cap. "I got dizzy walking on those stilts you made last summer. And I fell off my rocking horse when I was a little kid. I thought the horse was going to trample me. Landed on my head."

"I remember," Max said. "A good thing, too. You might have been hurt if you'd landed anywhere else."

"Are you going to walk that rope or are you going to spend all day making wisecracks?" Marty demanded.

It was a warm Saturday in the summer of 1936 and the Mitchell brothers were in the country, at the summer cottage they had named Honeywell. Their father, Harry Mitchell, was in town, working on an editorial for his newspaper, the *Indian River Review*. Their mother, Amy Mitchell, was in the kitchen of the cottage, baking a strawberry rhubarb pie. Earlier that morning, the boys had picked the strawberries and pulled the rhubarb.

Late in the morning, Max had persuaded his younger brother to help him set up a rope across the width of the barn. Max had climbed a ladder with a heavy coil of rope slung over his shoulder. He'd attached one end of the rope securely to a barn timber, walked along a narrow beam to the far wall and dropped the loose end of the rope through a hole in the barnboard siding to the ground.

"I give up," Marty said. "What's going on?"

"I'm going to tighten the rope," Max responded. "Then I'm going to see if I can walk along it without falling. I've been reading a book about rope-walkers. Thought I'd see if I can do it."

Marty shook his head. "Mom and Dad are going to kill you, Max," he predicted. "If they do, I want you to will me your bicycle."

"Did you say my bicycle or my old tricycle?" Max responded.

"Ho, ho, ho," Marty said without smiling. "My brother the comedian. Soon to be my *late* brother." He caught the end of the rope and attached it to the hitch of an old tractor Max had backed up to the barn. On Max's signal, Marty climbed aboard and drove the tractor forward until the rope was extremely taut.

"That's it! Good enough, Marty," Max had called out. "Come back inside the barn." He winked down at his brother, who stood with his hands on his hips. "Get ready to catch me if I fall."

"Oh, sure," Marty replied. "That's like asking me to catch a falling cow. You'd splatter me all over the barn floor. Wait until I get some hay bales to put under the rope."

While Marty was spreading the bales of hay, Max retraced his steps along the narrow beam. He picked up a long pole he'd stashed in the loft on a previous trip.

"You still may break your legs if you fall," Marty warned Max. "And if Mom catches us, I'll say it was all your idea. I had nothing to do with this."

"Oh, no. We're in this together. You're an accomplice. You helped me with the rope. And you drove the tractor. How long you think she'll ground us if she catches us?"

Marty groaned. "About 400 years, I'd guess."

Max just grunted. Then, steeling himself and holding tight to the balance pole, he took a deep breath and started out on the rope.

"Wait a minute, Max!" Marty called out. "There's someone coming! Hide!"

Max teetered on the rope, then stepped back onto a beam. He tried to hide in the shadows. Marty grabbed a broom and began sweeping the floor. A shadow fell over the open door. Whoever was outside was about to come in.

"Oh, my gosh," Marty exclaimed. "It's only Big Fella."

Big Fella was the Mitchell's prize husky. He'd heard noises coming from the barn and was curious. He trotted over and rubbed his nose against Marty's leg.

Marty bent down and cuffed him affectionately under the chin. "Okay, pal. You can stay. But promise you won't say a word about this to Mom or Dad. And you can help me pick up the pieces when Max comes tumbling down like Humpty Dumpty."

Big Fella wagged his tail in the affirmative, then looked up at Max, as if to say: *Even the dumbest of dogs would never try what you're about to do. Not even that stupid poodle in town, the one with a crush on me.* He sighed, flopped down in the straw and licked a paw.

Once again, Max ventured out on the rope. He took a step, then another. The balance pole swayed up and down, back and forth. Finally, Max steadied it. He took three more small steps, sliding one foot after another, getting the hang of it. His confidence blossomed and he took a few more steps along the rope. He was halfway across. He stopped, took another deep breath and found himself on a slight incline as he approached the end of his journey. Max thought: *The rope is not as taut as it should be. We'll have to make some adjustments before I do this again. If I do it again.*

"You're almost there, Max," Marty said in a soft voice. He didn't want to distract his brother by shouting. Big Fella didn't show any interest in the drama unfolding overhead. He closed his eyes and slept.

I can do this, Max told himself. He moved up the incline and reached out to grasp a barn beam. *There! I've done it! I knew I could do it.*

He sighed with relief. "That was really hard. I can't believe people do this over gorges and between high buildings," he called out to Marty. "Some have even walked ropes and wires over Niagara Falls."

"No kidding?" asked Marty. "That's one way to get from the U.S. to Canada without going through customs."

"Seriously, Marty, professional ropewalkers must have nerves of steel. They don't have hay bales waiting to break their fall if they take a tumble. One mistake and they're goners."

When Max climbed down, a triumphant grin on his face, Marty pounded him on the back. "That was incredible!" he exclaimed. "I didn't think you'd do it. I was getting ready to put your bones back together with hockey tape when you hit the barn floor."

Big Fella began to thrash and snore. He was dreaming of the stupid poodle.

"Let's celebrate," Marty said, fishing in his pocket, looking for some change. "I've got some money. Let's go into town to Merry Mabel's. Have some ice cream."

It was always busy at Merry Mabel's. When Max and Marty arrived, all the tables and booths were full. Then they saw Sammy Fox and Trudy Reeves waving to them from a booth at the back of the restaurant.

"Come sit with us," Sammy called out. Sammy was their friend from the Indian reserve at

Tumbling Waters, a village a few miles from town. During the past hockey season, Max had recruited Sammy for the Indian River hockey club. With Sammy playing a starring role and Max as player-coach, the team had won the junior championship.

Trudy was their neighbour at Honeywell and a close friend from high school. She was a horse trainer and harness driver. Recently she had won national acclaim by winning the Hambletonian at Goshen, New York—a prestigious harness race. And she did it driving Wizard, a horse owned jointly by the Mitchells and Trudy.

"Hi guys," Trudy said, sliding over in the booth, patting the seat, making room for Max. "What's up?"

Marty, who slipped in next to Sammy, began to laugh. "Oh, that's funny, Trudy. What's up? Max was up. Max was really up. Up on a rope. In our barn. You should have seen him."

Sammy and Trudy leaned forward, looking puzzled. "What in the world are you talking about?" Sammy said. "On a rope? You mean on one of those tightropes?"

"It could have been a bit tighter," Max answered, laughing. "But yes, I walked a tightrope across the barn. It was only about 40 feet across. And I was only about 20 feet up."

"And you didn't fall?" asked Trudy, impressed.

"Nope."

"But why, Max?" Sammy asked. "What prompted you?"

"I was reading a book about high-wire-walkers," Max explained. "I learned they're called funambulists, although there's not much fun in it as far as I can tell. It's a bit scary. I was curious to know what it feels like to walk a rope. That's it."

"And?"

"It's great. It was a big thrill. But it's difficult and dangerous. I wouldn't want to make a career of it."

"You mean there are people who do?" Trudy asked.

"Over the years there have been a few. One of the greatest was the French ropewalker Blondin. He amazed people by walking a rope over Niagara Falls. That was back in 1860—over 75 years ago. At about the same time, a Canadian, a fellow named Willie Hunt from Port Hope, Ontario, did everything Blondin did. And more. They had quite a competition going. They were big rivals."

"I've heard of Blondin," Sammy said. "But not much. And I've never heard of Willie Hunt."

"Most people haven't," Max replied. "He changed his name to The Great Farini. He was a remarkable guy. Wish I'd been around then. You know, to get to know him. To find out what it takes to walk a wire over the Falls, over 100 feet in the air."

"And with no safety net," added Marty. "One slip and you're fish food."

The ice cream sundaes arrived. Max smiled at the young waitress and she blushed.

"Marty's paying," Max said to Trudy and Sammy. "He said he'd treat if I made it across on the rope without falling off."

"Two sundaes," grumped Marty. "That's 30 cents out of my allowance. And I didn't even get to see you fall on your a...I mean your butt."

Sammy was deep in thought. Finally he said, "You fellows ever been to Niagara Falls?"

"We've hardly been anywhere outside of the North Country," Marty said.

"Now wait a minute. We all went to Boston for the junior hockey championships last winter. And you two have been to Ottawa—to meet One Eyed Frank McGee."

Max laughed. "That doesn't count. That trip was in a dream. Sammy, your chief at Tumbling Waters—Chief Echo—kind of hypnotized us and sent us skating down the River of Time. We'll never forget it, will we, Marty?"

"Never," said Marty. When he spoke, ice cream dribbled down his chin and stained his shirt.

"It was amazing," Max said. "Marty and I shared the same dream. And how *real* it all was. We spent the hockey season with McGee. And yet the dream actually lasted only a few minutes. The Chief and his friends, the Little People, put us in some kind of deep sleep. I don't know how he did it. It was uncanny."

"I know the Great Chief likes you two," Sammy said. "When you spent some time with us on the Tumbling Waters reserve, you did some things that really impressed him. He feels he still owes you. I'm sure he'll happily treat you to another trip down the River of Time—if you're interested, that is."

"Oh, we're interested," Marty said eagerly.

"You think he'd send us to Niagara Falls?" Max asked. "Back in time to meet The Great Farini? I'd sure like that."

Marty said, "I was planning to go to Niagara Falls anyway—on my honeymoon."

The others roared with laughter.

"Honeymoon?" laughed Max. "You're only 15. You haven't even got a girlfriend."

"So?" Marty grinned. "A guy has to plan ahead, doesn't he? And I haven't got a girlfriend because I just can't decide which one to go out with. Some of the girls at school even line up to ask *me* to go out."

"You mean they ask you to *get* out," Max said.

"That comment proves it, Max. You're really jealous of me."

"Enough," said Sammy, looking at the Coca Cola clock on the wall. "Listen, guys, let's go to Tumbling Waters and see Chief Echo. Ask him if he'll send you down the River of Time again. You can go in that birch bark canoe we made for you when you were on our reserve. It'll be the perfect way to travel."

They rose from the booth, but not before Marty spilled some more ice cream on his shirt. He wiped it off with a finger, then ran the same finger over Max's sleeve. Max didn't notice.

"I borrowed Dad's car," Max said. "We've got the whole afternoon. Let's go see the Chief."

At the cash register, Marty paid Mabel who said, deadpan, "Lose another bet, kid?"

Outside Sammy said, "I rode into town on my horse. I'll meet you back at the reserve."

"Okay. What about you, Trudy?" Max said. "Can we drop you somewhere?"

"No, you can't," she said, pulling open the back door of the car. "I'm going with you," she said with quiet authority. "There's room for three in your canoe, isn't there?"

CHAPTER 2

MEETING CHIEF ECHO

"Welcome, boys, welcome," Chief Echo said. "Come into my longhouse. It's good to see you again. You are always welcome on our reserve. You know that. You are honorary members of our tribe, after all. And who's the attractive young woman you have brought with you?"

"Chief, this is our good friend Trudy Reeves," Max said. "You may have heard of her. She drove Wizard to victory in the Hambletonian this year. She's the first woman ever to compete in the harness race."

"I have indeed heard of the remarkable Miss Reeves," the Chief replied. "Your name was in all the newspapers. It is a great honour to meet you, young woman. And to have you visit our humble reserve."

Trudy blushed. "Thank you, Chief Echo," she said shyly. "Max and Marty have told me many fascinating things about you and Tumbling Waters. But mostly about you."

Chief Echo beamed. "That is kind of them. They helped us out of a lot of trouble not long ago. Today, perhaps I can repay them, partially at least. Sammy has already told me why you are here." He poured hot tea into five hand-painted cups as he spoke and passed them around. "So you Mitchells are ready for another adventure, are you? Ready to take another trip down the River of Time? And you'd like to take Trudy with you? That should be no problem. I have already spoken to the Chief of the Little People. Has Max told you about the Little People, Trudy?"

"Yes, sir, he has. He told me that long ago one of your braves was hunting in the woods when he came upon a great ravine. And when he climbed down to the bottom he found himself surrounded by the tiniest men and women he had ever seen. Your brave gave them a pheasant he'd shot with his bow and arrow, so they invited him to dinner."

"And did Max tell you how the Little People controlled all the forces of nature? That their job was to shake the trees and flowers in the spring to wake them up?" asked the Chief.

"Yes sir, he did." said Trudy, smiling.

"And Max told her how they put them to sleep in the fall," Marty interrupted. "And I told Trudy how one of them picked up a large stone and hurled it at a large tree to show the brave that the

Little People were very strong. The stone shattered the tree and set it on fire. Oh, yes, another thing: they fed the brave from a bowl that never emptied and a cup that was always full."

Trudy laughed softly. She said, "Max and Marty told me the Little People are so shy they prefer to remain invisible. And how they covered Max and Marty with magic blankets and hovered over them when they went to sleep and journeyed down the River of Time."

Max said, "We know they helped to put us in a deep sleep and somehow we shared the same dream. That was when we went to Ottawa to visit One-Eyed Frank McGee, the great hockey star. It was a wonderful dream."

"It's good that you all believe in the Little People," Chief Echo said. "I know I do."

Marty spoke up. "The first time we travelled down the River of Time it was frozen. The smoothest ice we ever skated on. But it's summer now and Sammy suggested we paddle down the river in our new birch bark canoe, the one your people gave us when we were at Tumbling Waters."

"An excellent suggestion," said the Chief. "Did you bring the canoe?"

"No. But we can go back and get it," Max said. "I have Dad's car. The canoe is at home."

"No need to get it," the Chief said, smiling. "When we go to the small longhouse on the edge of our reserve—where you will sleep and dream— perhaps a canoe will be there. We'll go see."

Trudy raised her eyebrows in surprise, but said nothing.

"Sammy, you may go now. Go practice your lacrosse moves. Or your slapshot for hockey. Thank you for bringing your friends to me. They will see you later."

In the small longhouse, Max, Marty and Trudy lay on brightly coloured blankets. The Chief placed small pillows under their heads.

"Close your eyes and relax," the Chief said in a soothing voice. "The Chief of the Little People has asked me to tell you to think about nothing— nothing but clouds and sandy beaches and the waves lapping on a sunny shore. In a few moments you will be paddling your canoe, a splendid birch bark canoe that will carry you down the River of Time. I know where you want to go—to Niagara Falls where the water of the river becomes a great cataract—one of the wonders of the world. When you hear the roar of the falls, it will be time for you to beach your canoe. Don't hesitate or the strong current will pull you toward the falls and fling you over. On the shore of the river you will meet some famous new friends—Mr.

and Mrs. Willie Hunt. Mr. Hunt, as you know, goes by the name of The Great Farini. And you will see many fascinating sights. Now you will sleep. It will be a deep and pleasant sleep. Filled with pleasant dreams. The three of you will share these dreams. Enjoy your trip."

His voice trailed off and could no longer be heard.

CHAPTER 3

DOWN THE RIVER OF TIME

The broad river stretched out in front of Max, Marty and Trudy.

"The water is like glass," Trudy said in awe. "So peaceful and clean. I can't believe I'm here."

The three teenagers stood close to the shore of the great river. A fish jumped nearby and a bird swooped down for a closer look.

"It doesn't surprise me," Max said. "When Marty and I skated down the River of Time to Ottawa—which took us back to 1904—it was the best ice we'd ever skated on. And we got to Ottawa in what seemed like minutes."

"Look! The canoe is over there," Marty exclaimed, running across the sand. "Someone left it on the shore. Must have been the Little People. Let's climb aboard. Trudy, you sit in the middle. There's a cushion there."

When Trudy was settled, Max and Marty picked up paddles and pushed smoothly off from the shore.

Immediately, a strong current turned the canoe downstream and pushed the sturdy craft forward at an alarming speed. Max and Marty barely had to dip their paddles.

Trudy looked up, shading her eyes with her hand. "I actually thought this canoe had a sail," she said, laughing. "Or an engine. We're flying down the river."

"Sit back and enjoy the ride," Max suggested. "We're going all the way back on the River of Time to the year 1860."

It was a glorious afternoon on the river. The teenagers watched in fascination as major events from history unfolded on the shores, like movie clips flashing one after the other. They saw signs of the Great Depression, with people living in poverty, struggling to get by; they witnessed the Roaring Twenties when great athletes dominated an era called the Golden Age of Sport; they saw flashes of gunfire and primitive double-winged planes in dogfights over battle-scarred country as the Great War caused devastation everywhere; they saw the Wright Brothers fly for a few seconds in a flimsy plane. It was the birth of aviation. They saw men heading for the gold mines in far-off places with romantic names like Alaska and the Klondike, all of them intent on becoming fabulously wealthy. They saw a new U.S. president, a man named Lincoln, speak passionately about maintaining a union of states, thus hoping to avoid a civil war between North and South.

Suddenly, Max cupped his ear. "I hear it. The roar of the great waterfall. Make for shore, Marty, we're almost in the rapids above Niagara Falls!"

Max and Marty paddled frantically and Trudy screamed. "We're caught in the current. We'll overturn in the rapids."

But the canoe suddenly leaped forward, as if propelled by dozens of invisible paddles. "I think the Little People are with us," shouted Max. "They're helping us."

Amazingly, the current not only released them but it carried them away from the rapids and the falls. Moments later, to their great relief, it brought them gently to a sandy cove.

"Wow! That was some ride," Marty exclaimed, as he stepped onto shore. "Were you frightened, Trudy?"

"A little," she confessed. "Sorry I screamed."

"We'll have to climb up the embankment," Max said. "We'll hide the canoe in the underbrush. Something tells me nobody will find it there. And we'll need it when it's time to go back."

"How can we possibly go back up the river—paddling against the current?" Trudy asked.

Max and Marty laughed. "We'll leave that up to the Little People," they said in unison. "They seem to know how to get things done—even impossible things."

"We told you they control the forces of nature," Marty added. "I'll bet they can reverse the current and make it go upstream if they want it to."

When they reached the top of the embankment they looked around. In the distance, they could see clouds of mist towering in the air over a deep gorge, mist created by the descent of tons of water plunging over solid rock. Through the mist and somewhere beyond, they could see two cities, one on each side of the surging river. Both were named Niagara Falls, one in Canada, the other in the United States.

"I believe we're on the U.S. side of the border," Max declared.

"Hello there! Hello!" cried a voice from behind them. They turned to see a four-wheeled carriage approaching, drawn by two handsome black horses. The man holding the reins hailed them again.

"Are you the Mitchells? And Trudy?" he shouted.

"We are, sir," Max called back. "And who are you?"

"Why I'm Signor Farini—The *Great* Farini!" he said with a chuckle. "Everybody knows me. I'm famous. And this is Andrea, my bride." He stopped the carriage. "Come. Get in. Get in. The blasted spray from the Falls will soak you to the skin."

Max, Marty and Trudy squeezed into the carriage and, with a cry of "Giddy-yap!" from Farini, the vehicle lurched forward, bouncing over the cobble-stoned road toward a huge bridge spanning the roiling water.

"Signor Farini," Max said politely. "How did you know about us? How did you know we were coming to meet you?"

The famous man laughed. "In a dream, of course. In my dream last night some little men insisted I come here today. They told me I would meet two handsome young men and a beautiful young woman. They told me you were from the North Country and I would be wise to welcome you and become your friend." He laughed again and turned to them. "I think we'll become good friends, don't you?"

They crossed over the bridge. Max, Marty and Trudy were almost speechless when they looked to their left and saw the amazing cataract.

"Incredible!" gasped Max. "I've never seen such a sight."

"And some people want to go over that in a barrel," Marty marvelled. "And live to tell about it?"

Trudy pointed, her eyes wide. "What's that thing stretching across the gorge? Looks like a rope."

Farini turned and laughed. "That's *my* rope," he said. "The one I walk across. Care to try it, Max? I hear you're an aspiring ropewalker."

Max turned pale at the thought. "I don't know how you know about that, Mr. Farini. But no, sirree—no, thanks," he stammered. "I know my place. Twenty feet above the ground—with lots of hay to catch me if I fall—is my limit. I'm astonished that you do what you do: walking the rope hundreds of feet above the gorge; wind and spray to throw you off balance; huge crowds demanding you take even greater risks. That takes incredible courage."

"Look at how the rope sags in the middle," Marty observed, pointing. "I'm not sure I'll be able to watch when you walk out on it."

"Thousands do, every time I perform," The Great Farini answered. "It's how I make my living." He laughed again. "Sometimes my dear Andrea packs me a lunch that I eat while I'm on my rope."

Trudy gasped. "You eat your lunch? In the middle of your performance?"

"Well, I do get hungry," Farini answered. "Just like everybody else. I'm very lucky. I get to eat my lunch among the clouds. And I can throw my scraps to the birds. And the fish."

Trudy shivered. "How can you bear it, Mrs. Farini?" she asked.

Andrea turned and smiled. "Well, I'm slowly getting accustomed to the Signor's unusual profession. Sometimes it can be worrisome—like on a very windy day. But if he shows no fear, why should I? But one thing is certain. When I send him off in the morning I know he goes straight to work. And he comes straight home when he's finished." She tightened her hold on her husband's arm.

As their carriage approached the town the crowds grew thicker. And noisier. They heard music and Trudy clapped her hands. "Look! There's an accordion player with a monkey on a chain. The monkey has a tin cup and he's dancing to the music. People are putting money in the cup."

"And there's a fiddler and a juggler and an artist selling paintings of the falls," Marty shouted. "It's like a circus."

"It is indeed," Farini said. "Wherever you have a famous tourist attraction you'll find gamblers and pickpockets, con men and salesmen—all out to make a buck. They'll fleece you if you're not careful."

Men and women jammed the middle of the avenue and Farini had difficulty making progress. Many people in the throng recognized him and shouted his name.

"Farini! Signor Farini!"

Women blew kisses at him. Men reached for a handshake. Had the carriage stopped they would have begged him for an autograph.

"Where do all these people come from?" Marty asked. "Surely they're not all from Niagara Falls."

Farini laughed. "No, my friend. They come from all over the world. They come because Farini has promised to match the astonishing feats of the great French wirewalker, Monsieur Blondin. You're just in time for all the fun. It will be a splendid competition. You will see."

"Unless you are afraid to watch and close your eyes," Mrs. Farini said. "If you do, you will miss performances you will never see again in your lifetime."

"We are here," Farini cried, pulling the horses to a stop. "This is your hotel—the Imperial. And ours, too. Your rooms have been arranged for you. One for Max and Marty, the other for Trudy. Your rooms have new clothing in the closets and a bowl of fresh fruit in each room. I will arrange for someone to stable the horses while you go in and register. Go to your rooms and freshen up. Take a brief nap if you like." He pulled an expensive gold watch from his vest pocket. "We'll meet for dinner in a couple of hours. Let's say, six o'clock. Tally ho."

CHAPTER 4

FARINI'S CHILDHOOD

Dinner was in the Imperial Hotel's Grand Salon. Max, Marty and Trudy had never been in such a spectacular restaurant. Signor Farini tried to help them make choices from a menu the size of a bulletin board, discussing selections like "filet mignon," "chicken cacciatore" and "pheasant under glass."

Marty blurted out, "Hey, I'm not going to eat glass. Don't they have hamburgers on this menu?"

Andrea Farini looked puzzled. "What are hamburgers?" she asked.

Marty turned red in the face. He realized hamburgers were unknown in 1860. He said, "Oh, just some meat squashed together and fried on a grill. North Country people seem to like them. On second thought, I think I'd prefer seafood tonight—like the lobster bis...*bis-kew*."

Max cleared his throat, "Ahem, Marty, that's lobster bisque—pronounced *bisk*."

Marty grinned. "Sure, Max. Whatever. Or maybe I'll have the *quickee*."

"And that's pronounced *keesh*."

During dinner, Max couldn't resist asking Farini about his fascinating life. "How did you get to be a high-wire-walker, Signor Farini?"

Farini laughed. "I had a dream when I was very young, a dream my parents did not share. When I was about 15, I dreamed of a future filled with daring deeds, travel, and adventure. I could see myself riding a white horse, six shooters blazing, as I pursued a gang of bank robbers. I saw myself raking in pots of money in a high stakes card game on a Mississippi riverboat. I pictured myself travelling the world, amazing millions with my circus stunts and death-defying walks across a rope stretched high above their heads."

His eyes glistened as he talked about his years growing up on a farm. "Perhaps you have had similar dreams," Farini said. "One thing I knew for certain. I would not spend my life living on a farm. Lots of kids love it, like my friends in Port Hope. But it wasn't for me. I knew I'd never get rich and famous from raising stupid chickens or throwing slop to those smelly old pigs."

"Do you have brothers and sisters?" Trudy asked. "Did they have dreams like yours?"

Farini chuckled at the thought. "I have a brother Josh who is 18 months younger than I. When we were kids he used to tell me the way I talked reminded him of what comes out of the hind end of a bull. He said I'd never do any of those things. Then I'd jump on him and wrestle him and make him say 'uncle.'"

"I'll bet your folks didn't want you walking a rope," Marty said. "Mine wouldn't."

"You're right, Marty. One day when I was young my mother came looking for me. I was in the barn walking a rope I'd strung up between the beams and..."

"That's what Max did just the other day," Marty exclaimed. He stopped abruptly when he saw Max put a finger to his lips. "Please continue, Signor," Max said.

Farini gave Marty a friendly look and patted him on the arm.

"I could hear my mother calling me," he said. 'Where are you, son? You think those chickens are so smart they can open a feed bag and help themselves?'

"Through a crack in the weathered pine boards, I could see my mother striding toward the barn. Oh, oh. I would have to move fast. But I wasn't fast enough. The barn door flew open and there she stood, staring up at me, her eyes as wide as pie plates. Her hands flew to her heart and she gasped.

"I dropped the long pole I was holding and jumped nimbly into the thick hay that lay below. My mother gripped me by my overalls and pulled me upright. She shook me and asked me if I was crazy—was I trying to break all my bones?"

"That's what our Ma would have done to Max if she'd caught him," Marty interrupted.

Max stepped on Marty's foot under the table. "Sorry," Marty said. He turned to Max and whispered, "That hurt." Marty began to sample his dessert—a large wedge of chocolate cake.

"I tried to explain to my mother that I was walking a tightrope and that it was lots of fun. It was a thick old rope and I got one of the horses to help pull it taut. I told her I was really good at walking on it and there was lots of hay to catch me if I fell. Of course, I knew I'd never fall.

"Then I snatched up my long pole and scrambled up the ladder that led to the rope. My dear mother kept hollering, 'Willie Hunt, don't do this! You hear me?'

"She gasped as I took several strides along the rope. In a few seconds I walked completely across the width of the barn."

"Just like you did, Max," Marty said excitedly, wiping chocolate from his chin. "Only you took a lot longer than..."

"Hush, Marty. Let Signor Farini do the talking."

Farini was not fazed by the interruption. "My dear mother was so amazed she put her hands together and almost applauded. Then she caught herself. She took me by the suspenders and marched me to the back porch where we had a long talk. She told me she was really worried about me and my future. She reminded me that whenever the circus came to town, with its freak shows and clowns and wild animals, I spent all my spare time there. She didn't know I sneaked in."

"You sneaked in?" Marty asked. "How did you do that?"

"I made a clown suit and kept it in the shed. I painted my face and made a wig of horsehair. Nobody questions a clown. I'd walk right up to the front gate and they'd wave me through. But it was the trained dog act I saw that upset my Ma."

"Tell us," Trudy urged.

Farini chuckled. "After seeing the circus dogs do their tricks I went home and trained our farm dog to do some stunts. Soon I had old Bowser jumping through hoops until he died of a heart attack. Then I tried to teach the pigs to dance! And the mule to lick people's faces. When Reverend Smithers came calling, Old Barney licked his spectacles right off. Then Barney ate his hat. I laughed so hard that day my mother sent me to the woodshed."

Max, Marty and Trudy burst out laughing. When Farini talked of his life on the farm, describing an earlier era, it was as if he whisked them away with him and made them a part of it. They could almost hear the crunch of sharp teeth as the mule devoured the minister's hat.

"At the circus I met a strong man who influenced me," Farini continued. "Back at the farm, I began lifting axles and boxes of bolts for hours at a time." He rolled up his sleeve and flexed his upper arm. "Look at the muscles I developed. Other kids envied me because I was the strongest, most fit kid in the county."

"Wow!" Marty gasped, reaching out to press the bulging flesh.

"My mother wasn't impressed," Farini said. "Somehow she heard about the time I hoisted Jimmy Jenkins over my head, spun him around, and tossed him in the creek."

"Why did you do that?" Trudy asked. "What did Jimmy do to you?"

"He stole my baseball bat. He was a tattle-tale and a bully. And he was always picking on Josh. He never bothered us after that.

"My mother had noticed that I was always trying to draw attention to myself by causing a commotion, like the time I built some stilts and ran through the pasture on them. Those poor cows didn't know which way to run.

"My mother was right, of course. I did crave attention. I had set those cows arunning and abawling. Two of them crashed right through the rail fence in their panic."

"Was that the end of your stilt-walking?" Max asked, his eyes moist from laughter.

"Oh, no," said Farini. He paused to sip from his teacup. "My Ma never knew it but I got those stilts out late one night. I dressed in a white sheet and went on over to Jimmy Jenkins' house. I rapped on Jimmy's bedroom window and made some horrible moaning sounds. Scared him half to death. At school the next day, Jimmy's sister told me he hid under his bed for the rest of the night. They had to drag him out in the morning."

Gales of laughter floated over the table. Farini took another sip of tea and turned serious.

"Yes, my folks figured I'd grow up to be a doctor— a respectable man in our community. And I disappointed them.

"I told my Mom maybe I'd try doctoring some-day. I knew I was smart enough. But at the moment there was no bigger thrill than walking a taut rope. For some reason God had given me certain gifts. I often heard Him say, 'Willie Hunt, you'd better use these gifts and develop them. I gave them to you, not to your brother or Jimmy Jenkins or anybody else. Don't waste them.'

"I figured a gifted man deserves a great name. So I chose a new name for myself. I decided to call myself Signor Farini, after a famous Italian politician I'd been reading about. When my mother protested, I said to her, nobody's going to be impressed if Willie Hunt performs a stunt. But when The Great Farini does it, it'll be something really grand. Hunt's a good name but Farini's a great name. Farini's a name that says, 'Look at me, folks! Look at me. I'm someone special.'"

Dinner was almost over. Farini was donning his topcoat and silk hat, handed to him by the restaurant manager, when there was a commotion at the door.

"C'est Monsieur Blondin," gushed the restaurant manager, who left Farini to rush over and greet the famous Frenchman and usher him to a reserved table. En route, Blondin passed by Farini's table and stopped in surprise.

"So! Here's the brash interloper! The Canadian farm boy who wishes to push me aside, to steal my glory."

At first, Farini thought Blondin was kidding. He rose, smiled and put out his hand in friendship. But Blondin coldly pushed his hand aside and sneered. "You are no friend of mine, sir. How dare you intrude in my affairs! How dare you try to steal my thunder! Go home, I say, home to your pigs and cows!"

Farini's eyes narrowed and his face grew flushed. He moved closer to Blondin until they were face to face.

"Your outburst surprises me, Mr. Blondin," he said calmly. "I have long admired you and thrilled to your performances. But no longer. Now I believe I understand you better. I regret to say I find you to be a selfish, insecure and somewhat frightened man. That *does* surprise me."

Blondin exploded in rage. "What insolence!" he stormed. "What rubbish! Calling me selfish, insecure and frightened. Nobody—certainly not you—is more courageous on the long rope than I am."

"There's no doubt you have great courage on the rope," Farini agreed. "But I believe you are frightened of me—and what I might do to your sterling reputation. And you are selfish to think you alone should walk the rope over the gorge. You alone should keep all the profits. We live in a free society, Mr. Blondin, where competition is respected, not denied. The sky over the Falls is open to all." Farini raised a finger under Blondin's nose. "I suggest you concentrate on your own performances and not worry about mine," he said. "Looking over your shoulder to see what I'm up to could prove fatal, sir."

Blondin spluttered. "I never miss a step, Farini. But I can't wait for you to falter. I say emphatically, you do not deserve to be here."

Farini laughed. "But I do belong here, sir. Perhaps more than you do. Remember, I was born in North America. I live here. I don't need a visitor's permit to come here. But you do, don't you? You're from France. That makes you a foreigner, Mr. Blondin. A foreigner making a fortune off my countrymen. And you call *me* an interloper. That's rich. Enjoy your dinner, sir." Farini tipped his hat, turned and walked away.

In the lobby, Farini took a deep breath. The harsh words he'd exchanged with Blondin were disturbing, unexpected.

"I'm proud of you, Signor," Marty said. "You sure gave him an earful."

"So that's The Great Blondin," Farini murmured. "I must say I'm somewhat disappointed." He turned to the others. "I must apologize for the confrontation. Why not come to my suite and we'll order up some hot chocolate?"

In the suite, Farini showed the Mitchell brothers and Trudy dozens of his press clippings and talked about his many accomplishments on the rope.

He turned to his wife and said, "Andrea, my dear. I know you're about to tell me I've talked too long. I fear I may be boring these young people."

Andrea said, "You seem to have their undivided attention. Why not tell them more about your teenage years?"

"Yes, please do," Trudy said.

Farini reached over and took Andrea's hand in his.

"All right," he agreed. "I believe I left off where my mother caught me in the barn. She had seen how skillfully I had walked the rope.

"At the dinner table that night, she talked to my Pa about me. And she spoke with pride. She told him I had walked that rope so straight it was like I was making a beeline to the outhouse. She said the rope was glued to my feet. Not once did I come close to taking a tumble.

"If I expected my father's face to light up with pride, it didn't happen. My Dad—Tom Hunt—told me I was a foolish teenager. He told me not to entertain any fancy ideas about walking a rope over Smith's Creek or between high buildings. He said the crazy Frenchman Blondin must have influenced me.

"My mother stopped pouring her tea and asked, 'What crazy Frenchman? Who's Blondin?'

"'Blondin is the greatest high-wire-walker in the world,' my father explained. 'He's a little Frenchman who's creating a sensation at Niagara Falls these days with his stunts on the wire. He's insane to risk his life like he does. I'll wager it was Blondin who put all this ropewalking nonsense into Willie's head.'

"It was true. I knew all about Blondin. I knew his real name was Jean Francois Gravellet. I told my Pa that I didn't think Blondin was any greater on the long rope than I was. Or I could be, with a little experience.

"My Dad just grunted, unimpressed. Then he said, 'Willie, you're just a farm boy who hasn't accomplished anything in life while Blondin is world-famous. Everybody knows about his exploits while walking a wire across the gorge at Niagara Falls. He's a crazy man.' My father told me if I ever thought of trying such a foolish thing he'd disown me."

CHAPTER 5

IN A FARMER'S FIELD

"This is where I practice my routines and invent new ways to thrill the crowd," Farini said to Max, Marty and Trudy. "It takes hard work and practice to be a success on the rope."

He had brought them to a nearby farmer's field, chosen because of its isolation. Thick evergreens surrounded the field to keep curious visitors away.

Farini had arranged for a thick rope to be slung between two large maple trees, one at each end of the field. Farini pulled a long apple-picker's ladder from the grass, leaned it up against one of the trees and scrambled up.

"What's that you have in your hand?" Marty asked.

"It's an old potato sack," Farini answered. "Watch this!"

He sat on a tree limb and slipped the sack over his feet. Then he used his belt to hold the open end of the sack in place around his waist. He stepped out on the rope.

Trudy gasped. "You're not going to walk the rope in that old sack?"

"Sure am, my dear," Farini answered. "This will be easy, even though I have no guy wires to pull the rope taut. Sometimes I wear two sacks. The second one goes over my head."

"That would be impossible," Marty scoffed.

"No, not impossible, just a little more difficult," Farini answered as he began to shuffle along the swaying rope.

"Where's your balance pole?" Max asked. "Did you forget it?"

"Don't need it," was Farini's answer. "I can balance myself with my arms. Watch!"

He spread his arms and moved quickly along the rope. As he neared the far maple, his belt came loose.

"Oh oh!" he shouted. "Turn your back, Trudy!" Farini's sack—and his pants—fell to his ankles, revealing his white undershorts.

Quickly he leaned over and pulled up his trousers, then the sack.

He tightened the belt and laughed along with Max and Marty. Trudy giggled, her face in her hands.

"That's why I practice," Farini roared. "I'd rather

have that happen here than out over the gorge. With thousands watching."

He moved along the rope and reached the maple tree. From a limb he took another potato sack and placed it over his head and shoulders.

"Oh, no!" shouted Trudy. "You're frightening us. You can't see through that sack."

"No need to," came a muffled response.

With the sacks enclosing his entire body, Farini moved confidently along the rope until he had reached his starting point. The three teens watched goggle-eyed.

Farini stepped out of the sacks and called for Max to hand him his balancing pole, and a strange leather device that was next to it. Max looked at it curiously. It was a leather girdle with stirrups and suspender-like straps to go over the shoulders.

When Farini was handed the items, he asked, "Want a ride, Max?"

"What do you mean, Signor?"

"I mean I'll carry you across the rope—on my back. It's a short distance. And you don't appear to have much fear of heights. If you listen to my instructions, I guarantee you won't fall. And you'll be helping me because I may want to carry a person across the gorge one day. This will be a good test of my strength and stamina."

Max hesitated for only a few seconds. "Sure. I'll try it," he said.

Farini fitted the leather girdle around his waist and adjusted the shoulder straps. The stirrups hung down to his knees. He gave Max strict instructions before he allowed him to climb into the apparatus from behind, placing his feet in the stirrups. Max gripped Farini tightly around the neck.

"No sudden moves," ordered Farini. "Just hang on and enjoy the ride."

He moved gracefully along the rope, which sagged dramatically under their combined weight.

"Oh, no!" shrieked Trudy. "The rope is going to snap."

But the rope held and within minutes Farini reached the maple tree where he deposited his passenger. Max sat on a limb, wiped sweat from his brow and let out a sigh of relief. "That was kinda fun," he said. "But I'm not sure I'd want to try it again." He called down to his brother, "How about you, Marty?"

"You crazy?" Marty replied. "I don't like heights. If I tried that I'd wet my pants."

Farini shook Max by the hand. "Thank you," he said. "I learned something today. If I carry someone on my back over the gorge it will have to be someone smaller than you. A much lighter person."

"That's why Marty would be ideal," Max responded with a wink.

"No! No!" screamed Marty. "Not me. Get a jockey! Or a midget! How about a scarecrow?"

Farini shrugged. "As you like, Marty. There goes your chance to become famous. Well, that's enough for now," he said, removing the girdle and climbing down the ladder.

"You wouldn't dare try that stunt out over the Falls, would you?" Marty asked, his eyes still wide.

"Who knows? I might," Farini laughed. "Later, I'll show you some other stunts. And I'll give Max some ropewalking tips. But now, let's sit in the grass and enjoy the cookies and lemonade I brought from the hotel."

"Tell us more stories," Marty urged. "Did you ever walk the rope in your home town?"

"Indeed I did. I had been practicing for months for the big moment and I was determined to amaze my friends and neighbours with a spectacular performance. And I wore a splendid new costume, which I covered with a handsome black cape. Underneath my cape I wore a skin-tight suit of red, gold and blue. Gold slippers sparkled on my feet. My mother, an expert seamstress, had created the suit for me.

"My father looked in on one fitting and turned away in disgust. 'Looks like you're turning into a ballerina,' he scoffed. 'I don't know why I ever agreed to this ropewalking lunacy. Your mother talked me into it. You should be in medical school.' Then he turned and walked away, slamming the door behind him.

"My father's words stung and I felt my face redden. But I kept my tongue. Even so, I knew a major confrontation between us was not far off.

"That night, after Josh and I had finished our chores and just before I dropped off to sleep, I thought of my father's words. And I made a major decision. I would *not* follow a career he pushed me into. I pictured myself as a country doctor, wearing a white coat; working 20 hours a day; peering down inflamed throats or into the wax-filled ears of bawling children; treating overworked farmers complaining of chilblains, bee stings and swollen joints; prescribing medicine for their sick wives, women who could neither pay for the medicine or for my services. They'd figure a dozen eggs or an apple pie was payment enough.

"Then I imagined myself walking a long rope over Smith's Creek, or dangling by one hand from a rope strung between two buildings on Walton Street while thousands gasped and cheered my daring. I pictured myself high on a rope or a wire over the mighty cataract that was Niagara Falls; I tingled with excitement. I asked myself questions I could not answer: How do they sling a rope or a wire across such a huge gorge? How is it made taut and secure? How strong are the winds that sweep through the gorge? Are they strong enough to whip a careless walker off his rope and fling him into the currents below? Nobody in Port Hope could answer such questions. Nobody in Port Hope even knew that the fancy name for a tightrope-walker was funambulist. I did 'cause I'd looked it up in the dictionary. Someday I'd learn firsthand how much courage it takes for a man to be one—a funambulist—to step into space on that thin strand. If I go to Niagara Falls, I told myself, and I surely will, I don't imagine Blondin will be pleased to see me. Great performers who work alone don't like to share the stage. And while I'm impressed with Blondin's accomplishments, he does not intimidate me. From here, from the safety of my warm bed, I have no fear. But when I step on that never-ending rope swaying perilously over the gorge, a thin strand connecting two great countries, perhaps my nerves will shatter and betray me. Perhaps my body will begin to tremble at some point. Perhaps my muscles will tense and freeze, my vision will blur and my ears will ring. Perhaps I'll panic, lose all control and tumble to my death. Even if I miraculously survive a terrible fall into the waters of the gorge, people will laugh at me and call me a failure. I'll return to Port Hope in shame. Well then, I asked myself, do you still want to do this? Do you want to remain Willie Hunt, the spineless farm boy? Or do you want to soar to great heights as Farini the funambulist? The Great Farini! Yes, I said. I want to be Farini."

Farini shook his head, as if emerging from a trance. He smiled and leaned closer to Max, Marty and Trudy.

"When I turned on my hay-filled mattress that night, ready to blow out my candle, I looked up toward Josh in the upper bunk. I said, 'Josh, I've made up my mind. I'm going to Niagara Falls. I'm going to do amazing things on my rope. You'll be so proud of me. Everyone's going to be talking about me. And, Josh, I'm definitely going to give Mr. Blondin the surprise of his life. But first, I'm going to give the folks here in Port Hope something to talk about—something to remember me by.'

"It was then I realized that Josh was already snoring. He was fast asleep."

"Who cares about Josh?" Marty said. "I want to know what happened the day you made your first ropewalk in public."

Farini chuckled. "I'll never forget it, my friends. It was one of my best performances. Mayor Fogarty himself introduced me to the crowd. But wait. I have an idea." He turned to Max and punched him lightly on the arm. "Tell me, Max. These Little People you and Marty talk about. The ones with the magical powers, the ones who brought us together. Do you think they could take us back a few years to the town of Port Hope? If so, you could witness up close my stunning debut. You two and Trudy can judge with your own eyes whether it was a great performance or not."

"That's a great idea," Max said. "Let's try it. We'll have to lie back in the grass and take a brief nap. I'll ask the Little People to take us back in time."

They stretched out on the thick grass. A warm sun bathed their faces and a cool breeze ruffled their hair. Max made a silent wish to the Little People and soon he felt their presence all around the place where they lay. "They want us to sleep," he murmured. "And think of Port Hope."

Farini nodded. A slight smile crossed his face as he closed his eyes and recalled that memorable afternoon.

CHAPTER 6

A SPECTACULAR CROSSING

Max, Marty and Trudy mingled with a huge throng of curious spectators who were jammed shoulder to shoulder in the park next to Smith's Creek. The Little People had magically brought them to the small town of Port Hope, Ontario, on the north shore of Lake Ontario.

"Hey, there's a place for ice cream," Marty said, pointing.

"Forget it," Max answered curtly.

From the bandstand in the park, Port Hope Mayor Austin Fogarty spoke excitedly through a large megaphone so that every man, woman and child could hear. The crowd was estimated at 8,000 people.

"Ladies and gentlemen," he bellowed, his voice echoing off nearby buildings. "Remember this day, July 15, 1858, for years from now you'll be telling your grandchildren it was the date of the greatest spectacle in the history of the county. And you were here to see it happen! Yes, it's the moment you've all been waiting for—a death-defying feat by a local daredevil, our own Willie Hunt."

The mayor's wife gave her husband a frosty look and nudged him in the ribs with an elbow that knocked him off balance and almost dislodged his hat. "Of course I mean the *former* Willie Hunt," corrected the mayor, adjusting his bowler, "henceforth to be known as The Great Farini." The mayor signalled the crowd for a round of applause that was promptly delivered, generous and loud. Max, Marty and Trudy joined in and Marty whistled loudly through his teeth.

"Aw, he ain't so great," a voice rang out. "In fact, I hope he falls in the dern river."

Mayor Fogarty scowled and looked out over the crowd. He pointed a finger at the speaker, a round-faced teen with a surly look on his face. "You be quiet, Jimmy Jenkins," he ordered the youth.

"So that's Jimmy Jenkins," Trudy said. "He looks like a troublemaker."

The mayor continued. "Today we're about to witness an astonishing feat. Willie Hu...I mean The Great Farini...will attempt to walk a tightrope from the top of the highest building in town to the trunk of that old elm tree across the river. He's gonna walk high over the rapids of Smith's Creek.

It's a dangerous journey of 300 feet, and for most of his trip Signor Farini, our famous daredevil, who's just turned 18, will be 50 feet above the ground or water."

He paused and nodded at the leader of the town's brass band, standing nearby with his baton upraised. The band broke into a squealing fanfare. The mayor smiled and then shouted into his megaphone, "Now let's welcome the one, the only, The Great Farini!"

Farini stepped to the edge of a flat roof high above them and the crowd burst into a wild ovation. All but Jimmy Jenkins who brayed loudly—like a donkey.

"I'd like to throttle that guy," Marty muttered.

Mayor Fogarty hushed the crowd, asking for absolute silence, and then signalled the waiting ropewalker with a wave of his hat. Farini took a deep breath, placed one foot on the rope and stepped away from the building. With his balance pole swaying in the stiff breeze that flowed in from Lake Ontario, his treacherous journey had begun.

The Mayor turned to his teenage daughter Andrea, observing the way gusts of wind whipped her long hair across her face. He said, "I'm worried about that breeze. If it gets any stronger he may have to turn back."

She pushed her hair back and replied with a smile, "Daddy, I know Willie Hunt from school. Once he sets his mind to something he never turns back."

Now Farini was high over the fast-moving current. He thought: *I don't know why they call it a creek. Why it's as wide as most rivers and no place to take an unexpected swim. I see water splashing over and around hundreds of rocks that form the rapids. A missed step will surely mean a fall to my death. But I have no intention of missing any steps.*

When he was directly over the riverbank, a little girl in the crowd turned her head away and wailed, "Oh, I can't look anymore. He's going to fall in the water and be drownded." Some in the crowd chuckled nervously. They saw Farini stop and turn his head their way. He smiled at the little girl's mother as if to say, "Tell her not to worry. Tell her I won't be *drownded.*"

Then he moved forward on the rope, slowly, gracefully and deliberately. Suddenly he froze.

"Look! There's something wrong with the rope!" Marty cried out.

Marty was right. A strand of the rope, which was frayed and worn in spots to begin with, appeared to be coming apart. *Stay calm,* Farini told himself, *it's probably only one strand that's weak. If it parts, there'll be plenty of strength in the remaining strands.* The long rope had been borrowed from a schooner in the harbour. It was the best one available but its overall strength had not been tested.

He stopped and looked down on the crowd. He saw Jimmy Jenkins' fat head protected by a sun hat, his gawking mouth. "I'll bet you hope this rope breaks, Jimmy," he shouted. "If it does, and I fall in the river, can I count on you to save me?"

The teenagers around Jenkins laughed and punched Jenkins on his pudgy arms. One of them pulled Jenkins' hat down over his eyes. "If fat ole Jimmy jumps in the river, he'll create a tidal wave," the hat-puller yelled at Farini. "But we'll try to save you, Willie."

"Thanks, guys," Farini said, accepting the fact his former name would be hard to shake. He turned back to the task at hand.

A few feet ahead of him, the weakened strand gave way under the pressure and split apart, sending a shock wave along the rope. Farini flexed his knees and easily maintained his balance while hundreds of onlookers below cried out in alarm. They could see two strands of rope, each about a foot long, dangling in the breeze directly in front of the daredevil.

But the rest of the rope held firm. Farini stepped gingerly over the frayed portion and, without looking back, crossed to the other side. The stiff breeze hadn't seemed to bother him at all. En route to the old elm tree, he thought of the hundreds, no thousands, of times he'd walked the old rope in the family barn and how he'd prepared himself mentally and physically for any unexpected emergency. Now, in his first major walk before an audience, he'd encountered a worrisome obstacle. And he'd handled it well. *Perhaps as well as Blondin would have*, he told himself.

He thought of his father's words, uttered a few months earlier. *"Don't get any fancy ideas of walking a rope over Smith's Creek, Willie, and if you ever try ropewalking over Niagara Falls, I'll disown you." Well, here I am Pa, high over Smith's Creek. There's nothing you can do about it now.*

Willie smiled, putting his father's threat out of his mind. He heard the applause, saw the hats thrown in the air and felt the joy that comes with accomplishment. He allowed himself to exult in his triumph. It was a fine feeling to be admired and acclaimed.

On the riverbank far below, his mother, who'd been praying for him all the time he'd been on the rope, wept with relief. It was over. She dabbed at her face with a lace hankie and told the people around her, "That's my Willie up there."

A stranger grabbed her hand. "He's your son? Well, it's nice to meet you, Mrs. Farini. His name's Willie? Willie Farini. Strange first name for an Italian, isn't it?"

She said testily, "It's Signor Farini. And don't you forget it."

CHAPTER 7

FARINI LEAVES HOME

Tom Hunt turned and growled at his wife, "Let's go home. I've seen enough. Our son is an embarrassment to the family. He could be doctorin' instead of doing brash stunts like walking a rope. And you're the one who persuaded me to let him go ahead with it. Hear that applause? Now we'll never persuade him to give it up."

"Now dear," his mother replied, squeezing her husband's arm, "Willie looks wonderful up there. Look how poised and handsome he is! And what a lovely outfit! You know, Tom, he's got a gift for walking a rope. Nobody can do what our Willie does. And if we deny him the chance to make his dreams come true, we may lose him forever."

"I say we've already lost him," grunted Tom Hunt. "And I don't care if it is forever. Come on. Let's go home."

Their son's one-way crossing of Smith's Creek—later to be named the Ganaraska River—that

53

sunny day in 1859 was a sensational achievement and was greeted with sighs of relief and bursts of thunderous applause.

Only one onlooker, a teenager with his hat over his eyes, appeared to have something against the smiling hero. He pulled a peashooter from under his jacket and began shooting peas at Farini. His fellow teenagers mobbed the surly shooter and propelled him to the riverbank and tossed him in, fully clothed.

"Serves him right," Marty said to Max and Trudy. "Now can we go for ice cream?"

"Later," answered Max. "The show's not over."

What followed when the grateful Farini attempted to show his appreciation for the ovation he'd received was truly astonishing. Despite the poor quality of the borrowed rope and heedless of warnings from friends that a return trip might prove fatal, Farini stepped back onto the rope, threw his pole to the grass below and was soon back over the turbulent waters, his arms spread wide for balance. He stopped at the spot where the strand had broken, and it was there he pretended to lose his balance.

Thousands of horrified onlookers screamed as he fell from the rope, only to reach out and clutch it with one strong hand. His weight training enabled him to pull himself back on top of the rope with ease. Then he sat down on the rope and pretended to stifle a yawn, drawing a roar of laughter from the crowd.

His final trick had the crowd gasping again. For a few seconds, he hung from the rope head first, supported only by his strong ankles and his slippered feet. Many shouted at him, pleading with him to save himself. And when he did they breathed a collective sigh of relief.

On that July day in 1858, the handsome home-town hero won the hearts of everyone who witnessed his amazing performance. He returned triumphantly to Mayor Fogarty's viewing stand and borrowed the megaphone to express his thanks to the crowd for their wonderful support. When he finished his brief speech, his keen eye fell on the Mayor's pretty daughter Andrea and he felt a strange, powerful emotion race through his chest when she rewarded him a dazzling smile.

"Now let's get some ice cream," Marty said, pulling on his brother's sleeve.

"Too late," Max replied. "There's a line-up halfway around the block."

Farini's crossing of Smith's Creek made him an overnight celebrity. Several newsmen gathered round, including one from the prestigious *Toronto Globe*. They scribbled words like "stunning," "heroic" and "nerves of steel" in their notepads.

The *Globe* reporter wrote: *I came to this small town expecting few sensations. And I return tremendously impressed. I regard the young Port Hope teenager who possesses the heart of a lion as an equal to the renowned Blondin. He seems blessed with the same incredible stamina and courage. One thing the young marvel made clear to me today. He will not answer to the name Willie Hunt ever again. He prefers his chosen name—Farini. From now on, wherever he performs, he'll be hailed as Farini the Great. He's earned the right to that name, for great he most certainly is.*

Less than two weeks after his amazing feat, Farini was back on the rope in Port Hope. This time he wanted to carry a friend across the river—on his back! The friend, Rolly McMullen, was willing but the Mayor and several other apprehensive officials talked Farini out of it. McMullen was actually disappointed when his ride—and his moment of glory—was cancelled.

Because 10,000 had gathered to witness the stunt, Farini decided to give them an unforgettable performance. He placed a blindfold over his eyes and walked the rope. Midway across he stopped to turn a somersault. Then he stood on his head. More than one woman in the vast audience—his mother for one—slumped in a faint when it appeared for a moment that he would slip and fall.

After his second stunning performance, while he was accepting congratulations from the crowd, McMullen conceded that the officials had made the right decision in banning the attempt. "I know you are strong, Farini, extremely strong, but I weigh 160 pounds. The burden might have been too much. If you ever carry someone on your back it should be someone lighter than me."

"And I know just such a person," said a voice from the crowd. "I weigh 100 pounds and I'd be honoured to have Signor Farini carry me across on his rope." Farini turned to face the speaker. It was Andrea Fogarty, the mayor's daughter. Farini laughed and waved to the pretty teenager.

Fall and winter came and Farini returned to his studies. During the school year he began seeing Andrea Fogarty. If she had any qualms about his ropewalking stunts she hid them well. She urged him to follow his dreams and to achieve great things in life.

In the days that followed, his father, when he spoke to his son at all, urged him once again to give up ropewalking and become a doctor. "It's so much more respectable than being a performer, and far less dangerous. You've proved you can do it. Now give it up."

Their discussions became more heated and developed into arguments, with Farini finally stating he would live his life the way he wanted. "I'm mature enough to make my own choices," he told his father. "You put far too much stress on respectability. You think circus performers and showman are immoral, unscrupulous and depraved. You should know I'm none of those things and never will be. And stop hounding me about becoming a doctor. There are just as many immoral, disreputable men in the medical world as there are in the circus. Now leave me alone."

"See what a little adulation has done to you," roared his father. "You've become impertinent and obstinate. You refuse to give up a lifestyle that's bound to leave you either a cripple or a corpse. What's more, you're going to break your mother's heart. I've had enough. There's no place in the Hunt household for the likes of you. I told you I'd disown you and I will. Now get out."

Later, Tom Hunt regretted those words. But it was too late. His son went to his room, packed a suitcase, kissed his mother goodbye and left. He told Andrea, "I'm going away, out west to seek my fortune. Please wait for me. I want you to marry me. I'll be back within a year or two and we'll spend the rest of our lives together."

He wrote her from far-off Minnesota, where he stayed with relatives. There was a second letter and a third, always with a different postmark.

He'd been hired as a performer on a Mississippi showboat. On cruises up and down the mighty river he'd walked on wires, displayed his weightlifting feats and performed magic tricks. In another letter, he described what it was like to play the circus clown.

One letter to Andrea contained a newspaper clipping about The Magnificent Blondin. "He's announced plans to return to Niagara Falls next summer," wrote Farini. "And stun the world with his death-defying feats. We're going to be there as well, Andrea. Imagine Blondin's surprise when a complete unknown, a brash kid, shows up to compete against him for the title 'World's Greatest Ropewalker.'"

By early spring he was home again. He had money in his pockets, more than enough for a wedding. Farini and Andrea Fogarty were wed on a warm April day in Port Hope. His mother attended the ceremony but his father did not. "Of course I'm disappointed," Farini told his friends. "But that's his choice."

"And where will you honeymoon, Signor Farini?" someone asked.

"Why, Niagara Falls, of course," was the reply.

CHAPTER 8

MAX TO THE RESCUE

"Let's get down to the Falls," Max said urgently. He was talking to Marty and Trudy. It was morning and the teenagers had just emerged from the hotel. They stood on the broad veranda surrounded by people, all talking about the famed funambulists—Blondin and Farini.

"Look at the size of the crowd! We'll have trouble getting through if we don't leave now," said Trudy.

While they dodged and weaved their way through the gathering throng, Trudy said, "Wasn't that interesting? Sleeping on the grass and having the Little People whisk us away to Port Hope and back, seeing Farini's first walk on the rope? Poor Andrea. Imagine being married to a man with such a dangerous profession. I'd hide my head under a pillow every time he walked the wire—if I was her."

"I liked his mother," Max added. "But his father..." Max waggled one hand.

"We never got our ice cream," Marty grumbled. "It's your fault, Max. Why are you so interested in Farini's early life, anyway?"

"It makes no sense to come all the way down the River of Time to meet Farini and not learn everything we can about him," Max answered. "When I get home I'm going to write an essay for school about the man."

As they neared the river, they could see excited spectators filling every foot of space along both sides of the river. Extra policemen held them back from the lip of the gorge. The best vantage points had been fenced off and people lined up to pay steep prices for tickets to these places. People had brought picnic baskets and playing cards and books to read. They were there to witness the first confrontation between Blondin, the legendary French acrobat, and Farini, his North American challenger. In a bandshell in the park, musicians played lively music.

Max had been thrilled and honoured when Farini had asked him to be at his side when he began his walk over the formidable gorge. "A rope-walker never knows when he will need a strong pair of arms to help him out of a difficult spot," Farini told Max as they climbed onto the small wooden platform where Farini would begin his walk. "Chances are you will be merely a spectator.

But from my platform you will have a better view than most."

Max felt that Farini was overjoyed at the size of the crowd and was eager to put on a good show. "It was I who leased the fenced off areas, Max," he said, smiling. "You'll be amazed at the amount of money I'll earn today—even after I pay a percentage to Mr. Soper, my publicity agent."

"Hundreds?" asked Max.

"No, thousands," he replied. "Many thousands."

"Does Blondin share in the profits?" Max asked.

Farini chuckled. "No. He agreed to a flat fee for his performances. He's always done that. I preferred to gamble that a huge crowd would gladly pay high ticket prices to see us compete. I also profit from the sale of food and drinks. I even have vendors selling booklets about my life as a performer. I have learned to pay close attention to the business side of ropewalking. And it's making me very wealthy."

Downriver, less than a quarter of a mile away, Blondin was in a foul humour. He had envisioned a summer of solo performances, indulged in at his leisure and at his own pace. He was distressed and angry to find himself engaged in a duel largely created by Farini. Newspapers around the world devoted much publicity to the so-called "world championship" between the two ropewalkers.

"What can I do?" Blondin complained to Colcord, his long-time manager. "Until this summer the stage has been mine. At 36, I've spent years proving myself. What has this upstart Farini ever done? And yet everyone seems to be talking about him."

"You should not complain," Colcord responded. "You're the greatest acrobat in the world. It's only natural that someone would try to unseat you. Farini is here with his cheap rope, one that will sway in the breeze like a clothesline. You said yourself it's such a poor excuse for a rope that you would never set foot on it."

"It is a shoddy rope. Mine is much superior. And much safer."

Colcord said, "You've got to admit the two of you have drawn crowds like never before. Most come to see Farini fail. They believe he is doomed because of his inexperience. Their morbid fascination draws them here in hopes of witnessing his fatal plunge into the gorge—a plunge he can never survive."

"I suppose you're right," sighed Blondin. "They know I will never miss a step. Farini must be mentally deranged. However, those who come to see *me* will not leave disappointed. I'll deliver some thrills they'll long remember. And I'll perform some stunts that Farini can only dream of matching."

"There's a stunt Farini's planning that you should know about," Colcord said. "He's going to carry a second rope out with him on the wire—one over 100 feet long. He plans to drop this second rope down to a small boat—the Maid of the Mist—climb down it and then climb back up again. What do you think of that?"

"Impossible!" snorted Blondin. "It's not only impossible for him to climb down this second rope and get back up again, it's impossible for him to carry a thick rope looped over his shoulder to a spot halfway across the gorge. He'd stagger and fall under such a weight. I told you he's mentally unbalanced."

"Perhaps," Colcord said. "But I've been told he has tremendous strength. Don't underestimate him."

At noon hour of that day, Blondin gave his fans a glittering demonstration of his skills on the rope. High above the river's most turbulent place—Devil's Hole—he stepped on his rope carrying a small stove on his back. In the pockets of a large apron tied around his waist were some eggs. At the midway point of his journey he stopped for lunch. He lowered the stove and lit a small fire in it. He then produced a skillet, cracked open the eggs and cooked himself an omelette. He even saved a portion for his fans to sample at the end of his walk. Thousands applauded his unique performance enthusiastically.

Upstream, his rival Farini stood on his rope breathtakingly close to the Falls. His debut was equally astonishing and received equal acclaim. However, Farini's first few steps almost turned out to be his last. His long balance pole suddenly became snagged in one of the guy wires supporting his rope, wires imbedded on shore in cement blocks. For several seconds he teetered back and forth unable to wrench the pole free. His efforts resulted in a stinging leg cramp and people could see him grit his teeth in pain. While thousands screamed or groaned or simply sucked in their breath, only one decided to act. Max Mitchell rushed forward and gracefully leaped onto the rope behind Farini. Using only his arms to maintain his balance, Max started out on the rope.

"Go back! Go back!" Farini shouted. "You're an amateur. You'll fall and be killed."

"No, I won't," Max replied through clenched teeth. "But you will fall if I don't free your pole."

Max came to the place where Farini's pole was snagged and carefully straddled the pole, one foot on the guy wire, the other on the rope. Max looked down and fought back a wave of terror that threatened to turn his nerves and muscles into jelly. He willed himself to remain calm even as he was forced to watch the turbulent water churning through the gorge far below. He could not look away if he hoped to free the pole. Steadying himself, he bent forward at the waist. Slowly, carefully, his fingers outstretched, he reached for the end of the pole and caught it. Within seconds he worried it loose from the guy wire and shouted triumphantly, "There, Farini! It's free!"

Farini nodded his thanks and ordered Max not to let go of the pole.

"I'll steady it while you use the end of the pole to help you turn around on the rope," he instructed, his voice as calm as a stagnant pond. "Max, before you let go of the pole and turn back, take a deep breath. You are only a few paces from shore. Pretend you are in the barn, a few feet above the hay bales. The worst part is over. Tell yourself, 'I can do this. I can do this.'" Farini smiled reassuringly at Max and Max felt renewed confidence flow through his body.

He tried to smile back at Farini but his facial muscles were frozen in a grimace. He nodded instead, and then shuffled gingerly along the rope. Now Max was facing away from Farini.

"I can do this," he murmured to himself. "I can do this."

He paused and took a deep breath, his arms high at his sides. Slowly, a few inches at a time, he moved along the rope until he found himself at the brink of the gorge. A gust of wind caused him to teeter and he used his arms to save his balance. He could hear people screaming and he realized they were terrified he would fall. Inches ahead he could see the lip of the gorge. He shuffled toward it and then found himself safely past the lip. He began to breathe normally. Moments later, he fell into the outstretched arms of several men who pulled him to safety. Only then did he begin to tremble and perspire, his face the colour of the whitecaps far below.

The men eased him to the ground. Suddenly, Marty and Trudy were there, not knowing quite what to do but anxious to help. Marty held out a bottle of water that Max gulped down. His throat was as dry as burnt toast. Trudy fanned his face with a piece of cardboard she'd picked up. With her other hand, she wiped tears from her eyes using the hem of her long skirt. And when Max grinned and sat up, she hugged him tightly.

Meanwhile, Farini stood on the rope where the problem with the pole had occurred. He refused to move farther until he was certain Max was safe. The delay allowed the cramp in his leg to pass away. When the young daredevil was assured that his "assistant" was safely on shore and fully recovered from his ordeal, Farini said a silent prayer. Then he continued on his way with bursts of applause and shouts of "Bravo, Farini! Bravo!"

echoing across the gorge. He waggled his pole as if to say "Thank you, my friends," and moved steadfastly on his way.

By then, Max was on his feet and anxious to witness Farini's walk. From behind the railing, Trudy let out her breath and said, "Oh, I can't watch. Especially after seeing what you did, Max. Farini's old rope is slippery from the mist. He'll never be able to stay on."

"Sure he will," Max assured her. "He's the greatest!"

"I've got my fingers crossed," Marty answered. "And I'm shaking all over." He gave Max a worried look. "Even more than you, brother."

Max grinned. But what Marty said was true. Both his hands were still trembling after his narrow escape.

CHAPTER 9

TO THE MAID OF THE MIST

If Farini was unnerved by the swaying of the rope, dampened from the mist that swirled up from the gorge; if he was concerned about the sag in it, a sag that created a treacherous incline at the start and the finish of his walk, he showed no fear.

A *Globe* reporter, watching intently from the Canadian shore, turned to a friend from a Buffalo newspaper. "If The Great Farini has butterflies in his belly," he said, "he displays no evidence of it."

His friend replied, "What an entertainer he is! Who'd have believed that when he approached the far side, he would thrill us by standing on his head for a few seconds—an incredibly difficult feat."

Farini rested on the far side for a few minutes, then began his return journey. This time, when he reached the midway point, he stopped. He bent down and secured his balance pole to the rope with lengths of cord, then unfurled another length of thin rope he'd coiled around his waist. This rope was dropped into the gorge and landed on the deck of the Maid of the Mist, which was bobbing in the whitecaps. A crewman grabbed the rope and made it secure. Then the sailor attached one end of a thicker rope to the one in his hands and Farini hauled it up. Carefully, Farini attached the thicker rope to his main rope and tested the knot. While spectators screamed and gasped, Farini began a hand over hand descent of the rope.

He thought: *I'll look the fool if Blondin is right, if this stunt is impossible. What was it Blondin had said? "It's sheer folly to attempt a descent from the rope to a waiting boat and then climb back up again. No human possesses the strength required for the return climb. Any mortal who tries it— including young Farini—is destined to fall back onto the deck of the boat or into the unforgiving river." And what had Colcord added, "I don't think it's humanly possible for a walker to lug over 100 feet of thick rope, whether carried over his shoulder or coiled around his waist, out to the middle of the gorge. Such a rope is far too heavy."*

Farini smiled as he hovered over the deck of the Maid of the Mist. "Fooled you, didn't I, Mr. Colcord," he muttered. "Sir, you had no idea I planned to carry a light one inch rope and use it to raise a much thicker rope from the deck of the bobbing boat. But I can't take credit for the idea.

It goes to Max Mitchell, my new friend. It was he who suggested it. Pretty ingenious, I'd say."

Farini swiftly descended the rope and landed lightly on the deck of the Maid of the Mist. The captain and a number of passengers rushed over to steady him and shake his hand. Several patted his back. The first mate offered him a glass of champagne, which Farini sipped. After a few minutes, he smiled and said, "I must be off." He turned to a buxom lady standing nearby. "Care to jump on my back and come with me, Madam?"

The lady, already nauseated from the rocking of the boat, groaned and fell back in a faint.

The passengers and crew wished Farini well on his return trip up the rope. He winked at them and quipped, "I must go. If I stay much longer here I may get seasick." He handed his champagne glass to the captain, took a deep breath and then started back up the vertical rope. He noted it had grown slippery since he'd last touched it.

For the next few minutes it appeared that Blondin's prediction would become fact. Farini was forced to apply extra pressure to the rope with each grip of its surface. Only his great upper-body strength, the reserves of energy in his powerful arms and shoulders and hands, and a surge of adrenalin saved him from a catastrophe. At the top of his climb, he willed himself back onto the horizontal strand, his only route to shore and safety. And a future! He lay there, resting for a few moments, his hands trembling, his chest heaving, until he was able to get up, retrieve his pole and continue. Minutes later, grinning through the perspiration that covered his face, he managed to stagger up the incline and make a safe landing on his platform. He knew he'd just accomplished what no man in history had ever dared to attempt. And what he assumed no man would accomplish in the future.

On shore, Trudy said, "Is it safe to look now? Surely he fell. Is he dead?"

Marty had been peeking over her shoulder. "It's amazing, Trudy. He did it. He climbed back on his rope and finished his walk. I'll remember this moment for as long as I live."

The *Globe* reporter turned to his companion. "Blondin indeed may be the faster and more graceful walker," he said, "but Farini's descent to the Maid of the Mist—and his courageous ascent up the damp rope—was an astonishing act of determination, stamina and sheer grit."

His friend from Buffalo agreed. "I'm still sick with relief," he said. "During his climb up the rope one could see he was on the verge of total exhaustion long before he reached his goal. It was truly an incredible accomplishment. What bravery and stamina he showed! And what a grand ovation he received when he finally completed his arduous journey."

"We'd better rush off and file stories for our papers," the *Globe* man suggested. "The whole world will be waiting for news of today's events."

Farini had accomplished what many said could not be done. He stepped from his platform and made his way through hundreds of backslapping supporters until he found Andrea. He fell into her arms. She threw herself around his neck and cried aloud, "Thank God you are safe, my husband."

CHAPTER 10

A DARING DECISION

Two days later, the two competitors were back on their ropes. Each was determined to outdo the other. It had been impossible for Blondin to ignore his rival, and he reluctantly agreed the newcomer had style and skill and an abundance of courage.

"Farini shows some promise," he told Colcord. "But he's no Blondin. The strength he showed on the vertical rope climb was impressive and he's a world-class walker. But his exploits, I hope you'll agree, pale in comparison to my own."

"Indeed they do," Colcord replied. "You are still the master."

But in his heart, Colcord knew that Blondin could not have completed a rope climb up from the Maid of the Mist. He did not possess Farini's great upper-body strength. Nor had Blondin ever stood on his head midway through a performance. Until Farini accomplished it, no one thought such a feat was possible.

Colcord often thought of the good times he and Blondin had shared, and how the years, so many of them full of triumphs, acclaim and riches, had rushed so quickly by. Soon Father Time would tap Blondin on the shoulder and say, "It's over, son. Time to go. Quit before you make a fatal error." Colcord was sad when he thought of Blondin approaching the end of his brilliant career. Soon he'd give way to a younger, stronger man. Most likely that man was Signor Farini.

Colcord felt an arm on his sleeve. "Are you day-dreaming, mon ami?" said Blondin. "Come. It's time to go. I have something new to show my audience today."

An hour later, Blondin stood on his platform waving a pair of wooden shoes to the crowd. Then he slipped his feet into the shoes and started out on his rope. But the wooden shoes almost proved to be his undoing. He could not grip the rope as he could while wearing slippers. He began to slide down the incline of his rope. There was nothing he could do but try not to panic and to maintain his balance until the rope began to level off and he came to a stop.

His heart was pounding. His mouth was dry. The shoes had almost caused his death. *What a silly, stupid stunt,* he told himself. *Now what will I do?* After a few minutes' deliberation, he removed the shoes, turned and retraced his steps and managed to reach his platform where he changed his footwear. Angrily, he told Colcord, "Get rid of those shoes! I felt like a child on an icy slide and almost fell. The stunt was a failure and I'm humiliated. Farini must be laughing at me." He grabbed his pole and, in a foul humour, made a fast crossing of the gorge.

Upstream, an hour later, Farini mounted his rope. He too, looked grim and failed to deliver his now-familiar smile to the crowd below. Farini was thinking of the criticism he'd received for taking so much time to complete his previous walk. He vowed this time would be different. He started out with a rush, almost trotting along the rope to the cheers of the crowd. No one had ever seen anything like it. He made the long crossing in about nine minutes—the fastest time ever.

His next walk, one week later, featured a stunt that was so perilous it left onlookers weak with anxiety but, once completed, overflowing with admiration. Ironically, he encountered the same problem Blondin had been forced to deal with while wearing wooden shoes.

Farini had learned that Blondin had once walked his wire wearing a gunny sack over his head, one that covered his body down to his waist, with only his legs and feet protruding. Farini told Andrea he planned to surpass Blondin's performance. "My body, including my feet, will be totally enclosed in a sack," he said.

Andrea gasped and clutched his arm. "No, no, you mustn't do something so dangerous. What you propose is reckless, if not impossible. I want to be your wife, not your widow."

He merely laughed. He took her hand and looked into her eyes. "You know I never use that word 'impossible,' Andrea. To me, everything is possible—even walking my rope encased in a gunny sack."

Farini called Max, Marty and Trudy to his room. "I want you to notify the newspapers of my next stunt. And I want you to put up flyers on both sides of the river. Use my carriage. I'll make sure you are handsomely rewarded."

After much publicity generated by the Mitchell brothers and Trudy, another vast crowd gathered to witness the "Sack Man" perform. Fascinated, thousands watched in awe and terror as Farini stepped into the oversized sack. The opening was then stitched up and he was completely enclosed. Then he worked his feet around in the bottom of the sack. Using his hands from inside the covering, he pulled the loose cloth up and away from his feet, until he signalled he was ready. Max and Marty assisted him onto the rope and handed him his balance pole, which he gripped through the cloth.

"If he doesn't fall, he'll suffocate," Marty said worriedly. "I wish he'd stop thinking up new ways to kill himself."

"I do, too," Max responded. "As for suffocating, he had someone punch little air holes in the sack, up around his head."

"But the material that makes up the sack is too smooth," Marty protested. "It will slip and slide under his feet. Especially where the rope sags."

"I know he tested it on shore, Marty," Max replied. "Several times. He's too much of a perfectionist not to have. But it's not the same as doing it over the gorge."

Farini—the human sack—moved gingerly along his rope, cautiously working his way down the slight incline. Suddenly, he began to slip, as Marty had predicted. Like Blondin in his wooden shoes, Farini slid down the rope for about 15 feet. It was impossible for him to stop. How he was able to maintain his balance, no one knew. Only when the rope levelled off did he come to a halt. He stood there swaying in the breeze, the sack billowing around him like a sail. The next gust of wind threatened to send him flying off the rope and into the river. Wrapped in a gunny sack, there'd be no chance for survival.

"I can't go and help him this time," Max murmured. He shouted into the wind. "Come back, Farini! Come back!"

Farini heard the plea and nodded. He realized he was in trouble. He decided that he must return to his starting point—and do so quickly. But a hasty retreat was impossible. Ever so slowly he turned his body within the confines of the sack, until his feet were properly positioned and pointed back up the incline. Using his strong toes to gain traction on the rope, he persevered until he was safely back on the platform. How he made it back was miraculous. When he emerged from the sack, his face wet with perspiration, he grinned at the crowd and waved. "That was close," he conceded to Max.

"Give it up, Farini!" someone shouted. "Throw that dern sack away."

Max agreed. "Signor Farini, that stunt is truly impossible."

"But it's a perfectly good sack, Max," Farini answered, smiling as he fingered the material. "I said I would cross the gorge in it and I will. Otherwise, Blondin will never let me hear the end of it."

He ordered Max to sew him back up inside the sack. But first, he handed Max some special shoes. "Put them on my feet after I get inside the sack," he explained. "Put them on over the sackcloth." Reluctantly, Max did as he was instructed. "I still don't think you should do this," he pleaded.

"That's better," came Farini's muffled shout of approval. "Good job, Max."

Farini was lifted back onto the rope and made a slow but successful crossing. During his walk, he stopped to perform a headstand—still wearing his sack—while thousands shook their heads in disbelief. Others cheered until they became hoarse. On his return trip, Farini walked backwards, a feat that was much more difficult than it appeared.

The *Globe* reporter in the crowd scribbled notes of Farini's performance: *Signor Farini's backward walk, while sensational, was far surpassed by the image of a human sack traversing the gorge. Portions of the sack flapped in the wind while spectators murmured, "How does he do it?" and "How does he see?" There was no possible answer to the major question, "How does he stand on his head?" This incredible stunt took place during his walk. All were at a loss when trying to fathom how this great ropewalker accomplished any of his objectives. But accomplish them he did.*

When he emerged from the sack, while thousands cheered, Max rushed over and hugged him.

But the celebration was brief. Trudy brought alarming news. Andrea had fainted while Farini was on the rope. Some concerned spectators had revived her. They had called for a doctor and a carriage. She'd been rushed back to her room at the hotel.

CHAPTER 11

ANDREA PLEADS IN VAIN

The doctor was leaving Andrea's room when Farini, accompanied by Max, Marty and Trudy, reached the hotel and rushed up to him.

"Doctor, what's wrong?" Farini cried. "Is she all right?"

"She will be," replied the doctor. "She fainted from all the excitement, and, I believe, for another reason, too..."

"What other reason?" asked Farini.

The doctor smiled. "Mr. Farini, your wife is pregnant. You're going to be a father. Congratulations."

Farini was overjoyed at the news. He rushed into the room and embraced Andrea. He turned to hug his new friends. "I know it's going to be a boy," he said. "And we're going to name him Max. That is, if Andrea agrees."

"Max is fine with me," Andrea said, smiling. "It's a good name. But promise me something, dear. Don't

82

ever put our Max on a rope or a high wire. I find it more and more frightening to watch you perform. I don't want my son to follow in your footsteps."

"It's a promise," laughed Farini, kissing her brow. "We'll steer him into a sensible profession. Something safe. He can be a lion tamer or a crocodile wrestler."

"Be serious for a minute," said Andrea, reaching for his hand. "Listen to me. I've been thinking about the baby and us. Dear, it's almost more than I can bear to watch you perform. Every time you cross the gorge I shake with fear. I haven't said much about my concerns because I love you and want to support you. But now, with the baby...I don't know if I can tolerate the constant anxiety I feel."

"Are you asking me to give up my way of life?" asked Farini, frowning. "And the money that comes with it? I can make a fortune doing what I do. What would you have me do, Andrea? Throw it all away and become a doctor like my father suggested?"

"But the money isn't important," she cried. "It's your life we're talking about."

"Andrea, I am fully in charge of my life. I'm the best in the world at what I do. It's what I was born to do." He snapped his fingers. "I don't think I can abandon it just like that."

"But we're going to have a baby, a boy that might never know his father..."

"Nonsense," Farini replied. "He'll get to know me and we'll have wonderful times together. Perhaps in three or four years, before he really understands what it is I do, I'll retire from rope-walking. But don't ask me to quit now, not after the greatest summer of my life."

Andrea made a final plea. "But you keep inventing new stunts on your rope. You keep trying to outdo Blondin. There's no limit... I'm so afraid you'll..."

Farini took her hands in his. "Andrea, dear. Blondin is world-famous and I'm still performing in his shadow. When the Prince of Wales comes to Niagara soon, whom is he going to watch? Blondin, of course—the famous Frenchman. Not the poor farm boy. Soon Blondin will retire and I'll succeed him as the premier ropewalker. But I can't achieve that goal after just one summer. I need three or four years to surpass Blondin's feats."

Andrea put her arms around his neck and cried into his shoulder. "Darling, I know you are the best, better than Blondin any day. And I'm so proud of you. But I dread watching every step you take on that rope. And I dread having our child watching some day in the future when...when something goes wrong and..."

"Shhh," he whispered in her ear. "Nothing will go wrong. Let me think about what you've said. You know I must finish the summer bookings. Otherwise, I'll be branded a coward and a quitter. Then we'll decide..."

Andrea turned her face into the pillow. She thought: *I already know what his decision will be. It does no good to argue. Once a daredevil, always a daredevil. As for me, I must think of what's best for our baby. Tomorrow I'll write my parents. Perhaps I'll go back to Port Hope and stay with them. For I don't think I can survive the summer here without suffering a nervous breakdown.*

CHAPTER 12

ENTERTAINING A PRINCE

The day after Farini astonished the world with his walk across the rope encased in a sack, Blondin, his face red with anger, pointed a finger at his manager. "Harry, this is intolerable," he bellowed. "I won't stand for it. My reputation is at stake. Farini is driving me mad."

They were eating breakfast in a restaurant—scrambled eggs, pancakes and bacon—and Colcord tried to calm his employer.

"Hush, my friend," he said quietly. "People are staring."

"Let them stare!" was Blondin's retort. He took his plate and threw it on the floor. A passing waiter, carrying a tray of plates, slipped in the mess and fell backward, landing in the lap of a heavyset lady diner. Startled, she fell off her chair to the floor, taking the waiter with her. They lay there stunned, covered with eggs, pancakes and maple syrup and surrounded by pieces of broken china.

Blondin turned and admonished the waiter. "You should be more careful," he growled. Then he resumed his conversation with Colcord.

"Remember how we laughed at Farini and called him a simple farm boy. We thought he might wet himself at the thought of crossing the Falls. Look what's happened! He threatens to steal my crown. His sack-walk was magnificent, much better than mine. He's bold and absolutely fearless. We both thought he'd have made a fatal plunge into the river by now. But he survives and seems to get better with every attempt."

Colcord placed his hand on Blondin's shoulder. "Don't let Farini upset you," he said quietly, in an effort to pacify his friend. "Let me order you more eggs."

"I don't want more eggs," Blondin shouted, acting childishly. He didn't seem to notice that several diners were leaving the restaurant. Some glared at him as they made their way to the door.

"We must upstage Farini," Blondin said angrily. "And I know how to do it." He waved a finger under Colcord's nose. "Harry, His Royal Highness, the Prince of Wales, will be visiting Niagara Falls soon. When he arrives, we'll perform a stunt so daring, so electrifying that it will be talked about 100 years from now. The beauty of it is—we're the only men on earth who can pull it off."

"You keep saying 'we,'" Colcord said. "What do you mean?"

Blondin moved even closer and said quietly, "I mean you and me, Harry, working together on the rope. Two daredevils instead of one. On the holiday weekend, when the crowds are largest, I will carry you across the gorge—on my back! The Prince will be sure to watch our performance and totally ignore whatever that rascal Farini does. Think of the publicity that will bring."

Colcord gasped. "But...but"

Blondin raised a hand. "If I can carry a stove across I can lug you across. You're a little fellow. And I know you're not afraid of heights. The crossing will be a sensation."

"It would certainly outdo anything Farini might come up with," agreed Colcord. "He wouldn't dare try to duplicate such a stunt, would he?"

Blondin shook his head.

"He can't possibly duplicate it. It requires superhuman strength. He could look everywhere and not find a man like you, a small man with plenty of courage. Together we can manage this, Harry. Think how amazed and impressed the Prince of Wales will be."

It was a marvellous idea, a stunt so revolutionary it would stun the world. It would be Blondin's crowning achievement, a feat only he could perform. And Farini would be shunted to the background. He'd watch in envy as Blondin performed the stunt of the century.

"I'd love to see Farini's face when he hears about this," laughed Blondin. Then he sobered. "Harry, how much *do* you weigh?"

"About 150 pounds. Why?"

"Well, try to lose about ten pounds in the next few days, will you?"

When Colcord and Blondin told reporters about their extraordinary plan, newspapers all over the world printed the astonishing news.

The *Toronto Globe* reported:

Blondin to Carry Manager Across Niagara
Most Dangerous Feat in World History

Monsieur Blondin, the world-famous ropewalker and acrobat, will defy death once again in a walk over Niagara Falls on August 29. And this time the lives of two men will be at stake—his own and that of his manager, Harry Colcord. Blondin plans to carry the 150 pound Colcord on his back—an unprecedented feat! Colcord said he was looking forward to being a party to the "greatest daredevil stunt in history." He stated emphatically, "I have no fear and am fully confident The Great Blondin will carry me successfully across the gorge."

He added, "To carry a grown man across Niagara on his back will be Blondin's shining achievement and I feel fortunate to be that man. What's more, I know he is the only man on earth capable of completing such an incredible undertaking."

When the Prince of Wales arrived in Niagara Falls with his entourage, he went straight to Blondin and Colcord.

"My dear Blondin," he said, "I urge you to change your mind. Please don't attempt to carry Mr. Colcord across the gorge. The papers are full of the news and most people are predicting it will end in a dreadful calamity. I feel you are doing it because of my visit. Should anything happen to you both I shall feel responsible."

"Don't be concerned, Your Highness," Blondin replied. "I am quite confident Colcord and I will complete the walk. I could not possibly cancel it now without damaging my reputation. I hope you'll attend the event as Mr. Colcord has arranged some special seating arrangements for you and your party."

"I will be there, hoping not to pass out with apprehension and anxiety," promised the Prince.

Blondin graciously offered a suggestion. He said, "Your Highness, since you will be our guest, I suggest that you take the place of my esteemed manager. It will be a ride you'll never forget."

The Prince gave Blondin a startled look, realized he was joshing and began to laugh. He replied,

"My dear Blondin. How kind of you to offer. But I wouldn't think of depriving Mr. Colcord of an opportunity to gain the type of fame I already enjoy. The honour of crossing the gorge in such a unique way is yours, sir. You've earned it. As for me, if I want to cross, I can always take the bridge."

It wasn't long before newsmen gathered around Farini to get his reaction to Blondin's sensational announcement. "What do you think of it, Farini?" asked a reporter. "Is it possible for a man to carry another across the gorge?

"Of course it's possible," he replied matter-of-factly. "It's entirely possible providing the passenger doesn't weigh 200 pounds or more."

"Colcord says he's going to weigh in at 140 pounds for the trip across," stated a reporter from Buffalo.

"Then it'll be no problem for Blondin to carry him," predicted Farini. "Blondin weighs only 140 himself but he's very strong."

"As strong as you are?" someone asked, drawing laughter from the other reporters.

Farini smiled and flexed a muscle in his right arm. "To be honest, I don't think so," he replied. "For my size I've been blessed with exceptional strength."

"Could you carry a man across on your back?" asked the reporter.

"Yes, of course, I could," Farini answered. "And I will. If Blondin can carry a little man like Colcord across, then I'll carry a much bigger man over. The man has already volunteered and I've agreed to take him. It's all arranged."

This was an unexpected development, a major surprise. Almost in unison, the reporters shouted, "Who is he?"

Farini said, "His name is Rolly McMullen and he's an old friend of mine from my Port Hope days. Unlike Colcord, Rolly is a tall man with long legs. He weighs about 160 pounds. I'd prefer he was shorter and smaller but I don't know a way to shrink him. So far he's the only one to volunteer— except for my wife Andrea. And one other. Andrea was the first to say she'd do it. But she's too precious to me and I won't permit her to go. Besides, she's going to have a baby."

"Signor, you said one other. Who would that be?"

"My new friend from the North Country—a youth named Max Mitchell. He said he would do it if McMullen backs out. Mitchell is a well-built young man and weighs about 180 pounds. A little too heavy, I'm afraid—even for me. I might have to let him down halfway across and leave him to finish the walk on his own—without a pole. The young man may be brave—but he's not stupid."

Everybody laughed, including Max who was in the room.

"Isn't McMullen afraid to do it?" asked a reporter. "Most anyone would be."

"I wouldn't carry him if he was afraid," replied Farini. "If the man on your back becomes terrified, neither one of you will make it across. I'm convinced that Rolly will stay calm and do what he's told. He has no qualms whatsoever about putting his life in my hands."

Farini's statements created another sensation. Newspapers printed them in bold letters and people made plans to pack up and leave for Niagara Falls. They wanted to witness the extraordinary event—two volunteers riding on the backs of Blondin and Farini, as they crossed the most treacherous and slimmest bridge ever devised by man—a three-inch-thick rope stretched 1,100 feet or more over a yawning abyss. Two thin slivers of rope would be the only things separating four brave men from a horrible death in the boiling rapids below. One false step, a moment of panic, a strong gust of wind, the carried men growing faint with fear; any of these circumstances would lead to a terrifying fall and a fatal ending to the stunt. Such a bizarre performance had never been attempted before.

On the eve of the big event, the nervous Colcord came up with a brilliant idea. He bought two thick leather belts and a three-foot length of chain, which he attached to the belts.

"I'll wear one belt and you the other," he told Blondin. "Then if we do happen to fall off the rope, you fall to the right, I'll fall to the left and the chain will catch on the rope and save us."

Blondin smiled. "That's quite ingenious, Colcord," he said. "But unnecessary. You know I won't let you fall. Still, if it makes you feel more comfortable, we'll do it. Let's just hope Farini doesn't come up with the same idea. For we don't care if he and his long-legged passenger take a tumble off their rope, do we?"

CHAPTER 13
PIGGYBACK PASSENGERS

On the Canadian side of Niagara Falls, Max, Marty and Trudy strolled to the lookout situated near the brink of the Horseshoe Falls. There they gazed in wonder at the awesome sight. With each passing second, tons of water tumbled relentlessly into the huge gorge below, a drop of 158 feet.

"An old-timer I met at the hotel told me that over 6,500 tons of water goes over the brink every second," Max said. "And the brink recedes about four inches every year—from erosion." He pointed in the direction of Lake Ontario. "Since the Falls were first discovered, they have receded almost 1,000 feet. So the face of the Falls is always changing."

"That's amazing," Trudy said. "What else did he have to say?"

"He said that early in the century some very cruel people sent a bargeload of animals over the Falls—just to entertain the crowd," replied Max, almost shouting to be heard over the roar of the awesome cataract.

"Really? What kind of animals?"

"Well, there were some bears and a buffalo, a couple of dogs, some geese and even a raccoon."

"Did any of them survive the plunge?" asked Marty.

"The bears were the smartest. They bailed out and swam to shore. The geese flew out of the boat and survived. The others all perished when the barge went over."

Trudy said angrily, "It takes a twisted mind to come up with a stunt like that," she said. "Those poor animals. I can't think of anything more cruel."

"Would you believe me if I told you all the water in the river once stopped on its way to the Falls?"

"Not me," snapped Marty. "Look at it! There's no way anyone could stop such a rush of water."

"A dozen years ago, in 1848," Max informed them, "a huge ice flow jammed the mouth of the river and only a trickle of water made its way to the falls. People climbed down into the gorge and collected souvenirs, like muskets and bayonets— all kinds of things. Others rode around on horseback and engineers even dynamited some rocks that threatened to damage the hull of the Maid of the Mist."

"Wow! That would have been fun," Marty said. "There would have been lots of fish flopping around. When did the water start up again?"

"In a couple of days, when the ice jam broke up. People who were out on the rocks had to run for their lives. They could hear the roar of the water rushing toward them from a mile away."

Marty squinted across the gorge into the distance. "What I can't figure out," he said, "is how they got the first rope or wire across the river. I mean before they built the suspension bridge and before there were any boats like the Maid of the Mist to pull things across, like Farini's cable, for example."

"The old-timer knew about that," smiled Max. "Someone found a local boy named Walsh, a kid with a kite, and put him to work. They had him fly his kite as high in the sky as he could and the winds from the west carried his kite over to the American side. Somebody over there grabbed his kite and tied the string to a tree. To the end of that thin kite string they tied a little thicker string and pulled it across. Another, thicker string followed. In time, they were able to successfully drag a fair-sized rope across the gorge, and then a wire cable. Then they arranged a pulley system to get more cables across. These were spaced apart and ultimately connected. Voila! They were able to begin work on the first suspension bridge across the gorge."

"You're kidding me," said Marty. "Some kid's thin kite string led to a bridge?"

"Absolutely," said Max. "Walsh won a ten dollar prize for getting it there."

A huge grey cloud of mist rose from the base of the Falls and showered the teenagers and hundreds of other onlookers. Deep in the chasm, the sturdy Maid of the Mist was battling the currents, the boat's prow nosing ever closer to the base of the mighty cascade. On the Maid's deck, passengers huddled together, chatting excitedly under the hoods of their yellow slickers.

"Niagara Falls," murmured Trudy. "There's absolutely nothing like it anywhere else in the world."

Later that day, the two great duelling acrobats took their places on the high wires. Both appeared to be in perfect physical condition. Blondin was all in white; Farini was dressed in royal blue. He wore a gold sash around his waist and gold slippers on his feet. Both men donned kid gloves to help them get a firm grip on their balance poles. Less than half a mile separated the two rivals.

Thousands of spectators who had gathered around Farini's platform began to laugh when Max, using a large megaphone, introduced Rolly

McMullen to the crowd. Rolly was straight off a Port Hope farm, a gangly man with carrot red hair and a wide grin. He was wearing overalls and a straw hat. McMullen was not shy and turned out to be a bit of a showman. He displayed a sense of humour by feigning fright after he stood on the brink of the gorge and looked down. He staggered back and collapsed into Max's arms as if in a faint.

"That's a lot wider than Smith's Creek," he stammered. "Anyone want to take my place? How about you, sir?" he said, pointing to a man who weighed about 300 pounds.

The man shook his jowls vigorously. "Not me!" he shouted, backing away.

When McMullen pretended to look for an escape route, a way out, Max grabbed him by his red suspenders and pulled him back. Max wagged a finger under McMullen's nose and admonished him. "You promised you'd do this for Signor Farini, Rolly," he said in mock anger. "There's no backing out now."

McMullen turned to the crowd and winked. "Okay, I'll do it. But just this once," he said. "And if I fall, I'll never speak to any of you folks again."

The crowd loved him. One man shouted, "Good for you, Daddy Long Legs," a reference to McMullen's skinny frame and long limbs.

"Can someone lend me a bathing suit?" McMullen shouted back. "Just in case."

Downriver, Blondin noticed the commotion on Farini's platform. "Let's go! Let's go, Colcord," he urged. "I want to beat Farini across. Get up on my back!"

He helped hoist Harry Colcord into position and started out on the rope, inspired by the cheers of the crowd below. The wiry, lightweight body of Colcord created no problem for Blondin, just as Farini had predicted. At first it appeared to be an easy, uneventful traverse. Colcord kept his eyes closed and wore a fixed smile on his face at the beginning of the journey. But midway across, where there were no guy wires to provide support, the rope began swaying, at first mildly, then, as Colcord shifted nervously, violently. Blondin almost panicked. But he recovered and hurried to the next guy wire where he was able to rest for a moment.

Then the guy wire snapped beneath his feet! The main rope on which they balanced swayed drunkenly as people on both shores screamed. Perspiration filled Blondin's eyes. He fought desperately for balance. He shuffled to the next guy wire and ordered Colcord to get down. Without uttering a word, Colcord obeyed. Blondin's exertions had left him exhausted. Then, refreshed, he ordered Colcord back up. He staggered along the rope, inch by painful inch. Six times Colcord had to dismount while Blondin, gasping for breath, desperately tried to finish the walk. When Blondin was a few feet from the end of the rope, Colcord, his face drained of colour, shouted to the waiting crowd, "Thank God that's over. It was a nightmare! Hello, you Americans! We just came over for tea."

There was a wild burst of applause, and the spectators who'd been frozen in anxious, silent terror broke suddenly into a standing ovation.

"We've got something a lot stronger than tea over here!" shouted a stranger. Colcord slid down from Blondin's back, stepped off the platform, stretched his legs and then went over to shake hands with a number of spectators. A stranger handed Colcord a glass filled to the brim with a brown liquid. Without batting an eye, Colcord downed the contents with one long gulp. As he drank he noticed his hand was shaking. He smiled and held out the glass for a refill. "I really thought my next drink would be river water," he confided. "I was never so frightened in my life."

Blondin, meanwhile, was being mobbed by thousands of adoring fans. He chatted casually of his most recent feat of daring, as if it had been no more than a leisurely stroll down a country road.

He signed dozens of autographs and answered questions from the mob of reporters. He refused all offers of whisky and beer, but he did accept a glass of white wine, held out by a lovely woman with auburn hair.

Colcord, his face flushed, came over to embrace Blondin. "You are a fabulous man," he said. "I doubt very much that your rival Farini has the ability to match what you have just accomplished."

CHAPTER 14
FARINI ALMOST FLOUNDERS

Upstream, across the river, Max and Marty helped to hoist McMullen into the leather shoulder harness Farini wore on his back. Farini uttered a small grunt when McMullen climbed aboard and a much louder grunt when McMullen suddenly locked his bony arms tight around his neck.

"Ready when you are, Willie," McMullen said.

"Stop choking me," Farini growled. "I'm not one of your barnyard chickens. And don't call me Willie."

"Sorry, Willie," McMullen apologized. He loosened his grip...slightly.

"You're far heavier than Colcord," Farini muttered as he stepped from his platform and moved gracefully onto the rope. He and his passenger were just getting underway when Farini encountered some difficulty. The spray from the Falls was unusually heavy and it began to blur his vision. Rolly McMullen clung to Farini's back like a leech, his long legs sticking out from the harness.

"Relax, Rolly, you're throttling me," Farini gasped. McMullen moved his hands slightly and his fingers were soon digging deeply into Farini's shoulders. He didn't seem to know what to do with his legs. When he tired, his legs would fall and brush Farini's legs, causing the walker to pause on the rope. McMullen apologized, his mouth close to Farini's ear. "I'm sorry, Willie. My legs keep getting in the way."

"It's not your legs that worry me," Farini replied, breathing heavily. "It's your weight. You promised me you'd shed a few pounds. Colcord did."

"I tried to, Willie. Honest. But the folks around here have been treating me to free meals and free beer everywhere I go. I'm not used to all this celebrity stuff. Maybe I put on a pound or two..."

"Or ten," grunted Farini. He felt a tremble in his legs and stopped walking.

"What's the matter?" asked Rolly. "Somethin' wrong?"

"Listen to me, Rolly. You'll have to get down for a minute."

McMullen almost went into shock. "Get down!" he screamed. "Get down where? And how?"

"Do it now!" Farini hissed through clenched teeth. "Get down behind me! But be very, very careful. Loosen the straps to the harness. Feel for the rope with your feet and ease yourself onto it. My knees are starting to buckle under your weight and we're doomed if you don't get down."

"But I can't, Willie, I can't do it." He began to blubber. "We're going to die, aren't we?"

"Stop that talk at once!" barked Farini. "Stop it, I say! Nobody's going to die. I'm going to ease you off my back, okay? Get your feet on the rope, cling to my shoulders and you'll be fine. Leave the balancing to me and don't look down. I repeat— DON'T LOOK DOWN!"

Farini made it sound so easy. McMullen was able to fight back his fear and compose himself somewhat. He followed Farini's instructions to the letter. He found the rope with his large feet. Keeping his eyes fixed on the back of Farini's neck, he clung to him, his arms locked around his waist. His nose tickled. He ached to scratch it. But he didn't dare release his grip on Farini. Finally, he rubbed his nose on the back of Farini's shirt. *Willie won't mind*, McMullen thought, *even though it's a brand new shirt.* A few minutes later, he did it again.

"Sorry, Willie, I should have lost a few pounds," he murmured into Farini's neck. Then he added, "What I should be wishing is that I'd never met you. Then I wouldn't be out here with my fingers dug into your shoulders and my nose leaking all over your new shirt. I should be wishing I was home on the farm feeding the pigs and chasing the cows into the barn."

"What's that you're muttering?" asked Farini over one shoulder.

"Oh, nothin'," replied McMullen. "I was just saying what a lovely day it is for a long walk. And isn't it a shame we have to keep goin' in a straight line. And I wish my legs were a little steadier on this old rope. Are we almost there?"

"Halfway," grunted Farini. "Now Rolly, I want you to get up on my back again. I'm rested now. I promised to carry you over and by Jove I'll do it."

McMullen said a little prayer and, with Farini's help, climbed carefully onto his friend's sturdy back. *I managed that rather gracefully*, he thought, *despite the fact my legs feel like noodles*.

"Your legs are as long as my balance pole," Farini said. "Try putting them around my waist." When McMullen did, one leg accidentally caught Farini in the groin. He bent over and painfully let out a long breath. "Hey, Rolly, that hurt. Be more careful, will you?"

"Sorry," was all Rolly could say. *If I'd kicked him a little harder, I'd really be sorry*, he thought. *And so would Willie Hunt—I mean Farini...*

The long journey required McMullen to dismount two more times. His body weight sapped

Farini's great strength. No other ropewalker in the world—not even Blondin—would have been able to guide McMullen across the gorge to safety. McMullen's weight would have been too much to bear and the trip would have ended in disaster.

The last few yards were agonizing for Farini because of the gradual incline that led to the platform and terra firma. Even though his strength and energy were almost exhausted, Farini had no choice but to carry McMullen the rest of the way. By now the man seemed to weigh a ton. Step by step Farini inched closer to the end of the rope—to the safety of the platform. His legs quivered with fatigue, the veins in his neck stood out and perspiration dripped from his face, soaking his costume. Finally he reached the platform and fell across it. Eager hands reached out for McMullen, who tumbled off his back.

"Yikes!" shrieked McMullen as he slipped back and almost toppled over the edge of the abyss. Friends pulled him to safety. "We gotcha' Daddy Long Legs," someone yelled. McMullen fell to his knees and kissed the ground. Still on his knees, he pulled a large red handkerchief from the back pocket of his overalls and blew his nose—hard. Then he rose and went to help the exhausted Farini to his feet. He threw his long arms around the acrobat and hugged him hard enough to make Farini wince.

Wave after wave of applause greeted them when the ordeal was over. The spectators, most of whom had witnessed both crossings, recognized the greater difficulty of Farini's attempt, and rated his performance much superior to that of Blondin. This was yet another blow to the swollen ego of the Great Blondin. He had counted on world-wide acclaim for his ability to carry a man on his back across the gorge. But he could hardly savour his achievement when his rival was being hailed for doing everything Blondin had done—and more. What should have been his proudest day turned out to be a bitter one for the sensitive Frenchman.

Blondin looked on bitterly as the spectators raised their voices in a verbal salute to Farini. "The crazy Canadian has upstaged me again," he cried. He swallowed the rest of his wine and hurled the empty glass far out into the gorge.

Rolly McMullen realized his few moments of fame were over—and not a minute too soon. He promptly announced his retirement from rope-walking, which surprised no one, and said he was heading home. "But before I go," he told reporters, "I want the world to know I started to panic on the rope when Farini's knees almost gave out. I thought I was a goner for sure. But he calmed me down and convinced me we'd get the job done somehow. Farini's the most amazing man I've ever met. He even let me wipe my dern nose all over his shirt and didn't say a word about it. He's a real gentleman, ain't he?"

Within a day or two, after enjoying his role as an overnight celebrity, McMullen was back in Port Hope, happily feeding his pigs and cleaning the manure out of his barn. His friends and neighbours looked at him with new respect and admiration. The man with the patched overalls and the gangly legs and the funny red hair had actually cheated death high over Niagara Falls. Some of them thought it odd that several times over the next few days, McMullen was seen taking little leaps in the air and then landing on his big feet.

"Dern, that feels good," he was heard to say. "That ground sure feels good. No man should get more than a couple of feet off of it—ever."

CHAPTER 15

THE ROPES COME DOWN

When Max, Marty and Trudy arrived at Farini's platform one morning he was not there. A woman with a mop and pail was standing in Farini's place. She had a frilly bonnet on her head and a loose garment covered her body. Her stockings had holes in them. Her shoes were an ugly yellow. There was a brand new washing machine next to her.

"Pardon me," said Marty. "Have you seen Signor Farini? We were supposed to meet him here."

The woman turned and pulled the frilly bonnet off her head, revealing her face.

It was Farini!

The three teenagers burst out laughing. "What in the world are you doing in that getup?" Marty asked.

"Meet the Irish washerwoman," Farini said. He curtsied. "I've named her Biddy O'Flaherty. Today she is going to take my place on the rope. The people are going to love her."

He was right. Later that morning, when "Biddy" appeared on the rope with the balance pole, her skirts and bonnet billowed in the breeze. The washing machine was strapped to her back and the applause from thousands of spectators made Farini glow with pride. It helped that the manufacturer of the machine had paid Farini a huge sum to demonstrate his product high over the gorge.

"But if you lose control and my washing machine falls into the gorge, I'll not pay you a cent," the owner of the machine had said.

"Fine with me," Farini had answered. "And when I finish washing some clothes in your fancy machine, I assume you'll come out to shake my hand and bring the machine back." He winked at the man. "I'll introduce you to the crowd. You'll become quite famous."

The man's face turned chalk white. "You can't be serious," he sputtered. "I'll not be going out on that rope."

Farini burst out laughing. He slapped the man on the back and said, "I was just kidding you, sir. But the offer is still open. You'll have a lovely view of the Falls from my rope."

Farini—as Biddy O'Flaherty—promised to make use of the new washing machine and halfway across he—and she—did. Biddy lowered a pail into the gorge and drew up some water. Then she washed some garments—including a huge pair of pink panties—and waited until they dried. She beckoned to the people in the reserved seats, urging them to join her on the rope and inspect the quality of her work. Biddy shook her head sadly when there were no takers. She tossed her curls and took a deep bow. The applause that greeted the comedy act was deafening.

Standing on the boardwalk below, a man named Frank Soper led the cheering. Soper was a promoter and publicity agent retained by Farini when he first arrived at the Falls. It was he who had hired men to fence off a large area on both sides of the cable. Soper charged 25 cents admission—50 cents for reserved seats—and made a small fortune that day, most of which went to Farini. Soper had charged similar prices for previous walks and Farini was rapidly becoming one of the wealthiest men in the community.

"That was clever," Trudy remarked to Marty. "Farini thinks of everything."

Marty said, "I guess you have to earn as much as you can, especially if your next step may be your last. I'll bet Blondin is kicking himself for not doing the same thing."

The summer of 1860 ended and the chill winds of autumn swept across the Niagara Peninsula. Workmen showed up one day and Blondin's rope came down. Shortly after, so did Farini's.

Blondin immediately made plans to return to Europe where he had scheduled several engagements. He was billed as the King of the World's High-Wire-Walkers, although fans of Farini claimed he hadn't earned the right to that title. Farini attempted to meet with his rival before his departure—just to wish him well. Despite the harsh words exchanged at their first and only meeting, Farini was not one to hold grudges. He had long admired the brave little Frenchman's skill and wanted to tell him so.

A message came back from Colcord, delivered to Farini at his hotel. *M. Blondin sends his regrets. He is too busy to meet with you at this time. As his manager and long-time friend, I will be pleased to make your acquaintance at a time and place of your choosing.* It was signed—*Harry Colcord.*

They met over lunch on the following day.

"Mr. Colcord, I can only assume from your note that Mr. Blondin would prefer not to meet with me," Farini said, coming right to the point. "I thought he would have been curious about me, just as I am about him."

"Let me try to explain," replied Colcord, shifting uncomfortably in his chair. "Blondin is a performer with great pride. Obviously you have stung that pride this summer—and that angered my friend Blondin. It also depressed him. For years he's been known as the greatest ropewalker in history. And now, from somewhere out of the Canadian backwoods, comes a bold young man who secures a tattered old rope and places it not far from my friend Blondin's. Then this young, uh, interloper proceeds to equal or surpass many of Blondin's greatest stunts. It was a terrible blow to his ego when you did that, Farini. At times you made an extraordinary performer look, well, rather ordinary. Some people even taunted him, saying he was no longer the king. They said he was getting old and had lost his courage and should retire."

"But in my opinion most of the people who came here this summer loved us equally well," replied Farini. "Some may have preferred his performances, others may have been lured to mine. Surely there was enough applause—and certainly financial reward—for us both."

"Ah, you bring up another sore point," said Colcord. "Financial gain. Once more it appears that you've outsmarted us. For years Blondin has placed his performances first, and finances second. He was quite content to perform for an agreed-upon fee. You have far surpassed his earnings by leasing ideal vantage points and charging admission."

"That was his choice," said Farini. "Personally, I believe in good old American enterprise. If I'm going to risk my life on the wire, I want people to pay for it. And pay handsomely."

"Oh, I quite agree," said Colcord. "I know you made an excellent arrangement with Mr. Soper, the promoter. And didn't you insist that the operators of the Maid of the Mist pay you a fee for each passenger who witnessed your performances from the gorge?"

"I did indeed, Mr. Colcord. Why did you and Blondin not do the same? Did you not think of it?"

Colcord twisted his napkin. "No, sir. I must confess we did not. I suppose we are more dreamers than businessmen. I must compliment you on your shrewd deal. May I ask, now that the season is over, what you earned on some of your walks from these various sources of revenue."

Farini hesitated. Then he said, "Normally, I would not divulge my earnings, Mr. Colcord. But what I'm willing to reveal may be helpful to you and Blondin in the future. I can tell you that my walk with McMullen on my back netted me about 15,000 dollars."

Colcord recoiled in shock. "Oh, my goodness," he gulped. "That's an amazing amount. I never dreamed... I'll know better how to make my friend's future performances more profitable. I do thank you for this valuable information. Monsieur Blondin may not agree with me, but I consider you to be a wonderful rival and a great gentleman. You are a splendid chap, Farini, simply splendid. Thank you again."

"You're most welcome, Mr. Colcord. I respect you for the courage you showed in crossing on his back. And tell my rival Blondin not to retire just yet. He's still one of the greatest entertainers on earth."

"He is feeling very blue just now," Colcord sighed. "He knows you bested him this summer, and when the crowd turned ugly, calling him a 'has-been' and 'second-best,' it went straight to his heart. It left him devastated."

"But Blondin is a marvellous champion," said Farini, "He's a legend and he always will be..."

"We both know that," answered Colcord, beaming at the compliment. "But he feels like a failure. Farini, you are young and have great confidence in yourself. But how will you react on the day the crowd turns on you? You may feel exactly like Blondin does today."

"Oh, I doubt that," laughed Farini. "First, why would the crowd turn on me? They love the thrills I provide. They come from distant countries to see me perform. They pay good money for choice seats and often bring me gifts. Some want me to leave my wife and marry their daughters. I am living the great American dream, Mr. Colcord. I hope it never ends."

"But it will end—someday," said Colcord earnestly. "And I hope you will be able to deal with it when the adulation, the glory and possibly the money too, is all gone. I worry about you, like I do Blondin. How will men like you handle the future when there are no more challenges to face, no more wires or ropes to walk?"

"I don't know about your friend Blondin, Mr. Colcord, but I will find new challenges if it comes to that. But I think it unlikely. I walk ropes and wires. It's what I do best. It's what I was born to do. I'll be walking high above the crowds when I'm an old man. And as for the crowd turning on me, sir, I doubt that will ever happen."

When he returned to his room, Farini found Andrea in a happy mood. She was humming a popular song as she took several frocks from the closet and neatly folded them into a large travel trunk.

"My dear, what are you doing?" asked Farini.

"I'm packing, hon. The summer's finally over and your rope has come down. We can go home now. You said we could. My parents have written me. They've asked us to visit."

Farini frowned and rubbed his chin. "But Andrea, my work is not quite finished here. I'm committed to one final performance. Did I not tell you that?"

Andrea turned from the trunk and the look on her face was one of surprise and shock. "No," she said. "You didn't tell me. I thought...but your rope has come down. What kind of performance did you agree to? Is it weightlifting? Is it magic?" Her lower lip began to quiver and a tear spilled down her cheek.

Farini frowned. How could he tell her about his final performance of the season?

The arrangements had been made only yesterday, after he'd led her to believe they'd be leaving when his rope came down. He knew why he hadn't said anything. It was because he knew she'd be bitterly disappointed and angry. And he knew, deep inside, he was being selfish. He wanted one final moment of glory, one more opportunity to amaze the crowds with his brilliance. Now he'd given his word to Frank Soper and the handbills announcing his plans were out in the streets. They read, "Farini Ends Season With a Perilous Stunt" and "Daredevil to Attempt the Impossible."

He cleared his throat and said, "Andrea, dear, I will not lie to you. Yesterday I agreed to stay a few more days and give a final performance on Saturday. It's a brilliant stunt, one so original that, of all the people on earth, only I can do it. I must do this, even if it means you'll be angry with me."

She said, "But you did lie to me. You led me to believe we were through here. Yes, I'm angry. And I'm hurt and disappointed, too. Just when I think the season is over it's not over. Saturday will come and then you'll tell me something else has come along to keep us here even longer. There'll be one *more* stunt, one more round of applause, a few more hundred dollars."

"No, no," he protested. "We'll leave on Sunday. I promise..."

Andrea folded her arms and shook her head. "You don't seem to care how I feel, or how desperately I want you to quit this work."

He threw out his arms. "Andrea, we've talked about this many times. In three or four years I can give it up. But not just now."

She looked her husband in the eye. "What time is this...this...grand finale of yours on Saturday?"

He said, "It's scheduled for four in the afternoon."

"There's a carriage leaving for Port Hope on Saturday morning," she said. "I plan to be on it. I promised my parents I'd come and visit. Unlike you, I keep my promises. Perhaps when you finish this final stunt you'll come to Port Hope. Or perhaps some other attractive offer will come up and keep you here. I've made up my mind to go. It looks like you've made up your mind to stay." She moved to the bed and began folding another gown.

Farini felt miserable. He hadn't meant to hurt her, hadn't meant to let her down. It had been a glorious summer, one filled with memorable triumphs. And his greatest accomplishment lay just ahead—on Saturday afternoon. He had planned a blockbuster stunt—one the whole world would pause to marvel at.

He thought, *I need Andrea, need her badly. But I also need the adoration of the crowd. I also need respect, the kind of respect my father said I'd never earn. Well, I have earned respect and I savour it.*

I never felt more alive, more energized, than when I challenged danger and death high above the gorge. Should I sacrifice all the glory I've sought and won, and the fortune I'm accumulating? Should I allow the gifts God has given me—the strength, the incredible balance—to deteriorate and erode? Am I willing to abandon my unique niche in the world, a world of posh hotels and fine restaurants and handsome payments—after just one season? For what? A return to the farm? No, I could never be a farmer. I would turn as sour as old milk, as surly as a man with a thorn in his foot.

Be honest, Farini. As much as you love Andrea, what sense does it make to quit while you're on top? Why walk away while you're on the verge of becoming one of the greatest performers in history?

No, he told himself, *that doesn't make sense. No sense at all.*

"Andrea, I don't have a choice," he heard himself say. "I must stay."

CHAPTER 16

ON THE BRINK OF DEATH

Farini's brow wrinkled into a frown as he approached the steep bank of one of the world's most famous rivers. Looking down, he saw an overwhelming mass of turbulent water rushing toward the brink of the American Falls, and a thrill went up his spine. Did he really intend to wade into that treacherous current? Would it knock him over like a splinter and fling him over the cataract? Or would he—could he—become the first human to walk across the very brink of the Falls? Off to his right, plummeting over the lip of the Falls, 150,000 tons of wild water disappeared each second, arcing in a foamy fall to the pile of rocks waiting below. As it raced by at Farini's feet, the cascade roared as if in protest to the inevitable plunge, a centuries-old howl that could be heard for miles downstream.

Max took Farini by the arm. "Let's go back, Signor," he urged. Anything you plan to do here is obviously impossible. Marty and Trudy are so frightened for you they can barely speak. I am, too."

Farini gazed into his young friend's eyes. It was true that he was dealing with the great unknown. The exhilarating tingle of excitement he always felt when embarking on a new and dangerous venture was missing. In its place was a feeling of anxiety, a strange sensation that something was amiss. Was it a premonition that something might go terribly wrong? It was a new sensation. He tried to rinse it from his mind.

"Tell your friends that there is nothing to fear," he told Max. "I will wade into the Falls on my stilts and come safely out of the water on the far side of the river."

"Stilts?" barked Max. "Stilts will snap like matchsticks when the current hits them. You'll be swept away in an instant."

"No, Max," Farini said. "I'll be on solid metal stilts. Unbreakable stilts. Strapped on. And I'll have a metal pole to assist me. The rushing water will swirl around and past them. The stilts will keep most of my body above the surface. It would be suicide to attempt a crossing any other way."

"But what if the water is deeper in the middle— deeper than you think? What if you dislodge a rock with your pole and you lose your balance? What if you step in a hole and go down."

"I am certain it is not over three feet deep in any one place. Four at the most," Farini answered. "And I've been told the river bed is flat." He laughed. "Max, my boy, if you are so concerned for my safety, why don't you take a stick and go out and measure the depth for me."

Max shuddered. "No, thanks, Signor. I just hope you're right. But I fear a disaster."

Farini walked a few paces along the riverbank and began stretching, loosening up. He was warming up for the trial ahead. His body was in superb shape. But his mind...?

Was he dwelling too much on Andrea and their parting? Was it because he was about to attempt a death-defying stunt at ground level and not 100 feet in the air where he felt so comfortable and secure? He did not know why the customary elation he felt was missing. In its place was sadness and apprehension.

In a few moments he would challenge the mighty river and perform the most terrifying feat ever conceived by man, a feat so bold and hazardous that no other man on earth would dare to attempt it.

He stood there on the shore of the Niagara River, gazing into the swirling blue-green current. Somewhere he heard a distant voice, a growling, snarling voice, which seemed to be rooted in the roiling, roaring water. Was the river mocking him?

Try me, Farini, it seemed to say, *I dare you. Put one foot in me and I'll snap it off. Try to cross me and I'll dash you to pieces on my rocks. Just try me, Farini, you stubborn fool. I'm mean and I'm angry and no man has ever tamed me. I dare you to invade me, Farini. They'll find your battered body and your pitiful stilts on the rocks below my precipice.*

The voice sent chills surging up Farini's spine, but he willed the growls from the river to cease, and they did. He willed his backbone to be strong and steady and the chills disappeared. He willed himself to be braver than he'd ever been before and from somewhere in his being, emerging from his body's resources, came courage and confidence and faith—all the attributes he would need to complete the daunting challenge ahead.

Then he thought of Andrea. When she had learned what he proposed to do—to walk on stilts across the brink of the American Falls, that there was no changing his mind—she had fallen on the bed, sobbing inconsolably.

"I can't bear the thought of such a thing," she had cried. "And I won't watch you do it. It would drive me insane to witness it. I can't! I won't!"

Farini lay down beside her. He stroked her golden hair and put his head close to hers. In a soothing voice he said, "Andrea, nothing will go wrong, I assure you. And anyway, you know I can't back out. The crowds are arriving. I can't disappoint my loyal fans."

"Your fans are not loyal," she said between sobs. "They are bloodthirsty and morbid. Most come to see you fail, not to applaud your success. I've been among them when you perform. Some of them are barbaric. They want to be able to say, 'I was there when The Great Farini fell.' "

"Nevertheless, Andrea, I promised I would walk across the river above the American Falls on a pair of stilts and that's what I shall do."

"But nobody has ever done such a thing before," she protested. "You have no idea of the strength of the current above the Falls. And those stilts! They'll be swept out from under you in an instant."

Farini kissed the back of her neck. "Dear, this will be my last stunt of the season. Next year I'll go back to my high wire act where you know I'm always in control. Walking above the Falls is risky, of course. But the crowd demands something different each time, something a little more dangerous, and only I can deliver it."

"The crowd!" she cried, rising to her feet. "All those foolish men and women. What about me? What about our baby? I could be a widow in a matter of hours and you talk about the crowd. Thousands of ignorant thrill-seekers paying 25 cents in hopes of seeing you get crushed to death when you go over the Falls."

Farini sat up on the bed and sighed. It was a conversation similar to many they'd had in the past.

"Andrea," he began.

She put up a hand. "No more," she said. She dried her eyes. It was over. Her bags, packed the night before, were in the hotel lobby. She gathered the rest of her personal effects and walked from the room. Farini trailed behind her.

The carriage arrived and the driver took charge of her belongings. She turned to Farini and they embraced. She said, "Husband, I don't want to cry over you anymore. I dread what might happen today so I won't be there. I desired a lifetime of happiness with you, not pain. I'll always love you but I must leave you now. I must."

Then she was gone.

CHAPTER 17

STUCK IN THE RAGING RIVER

The burly blacksmith hesitated when he approached Farini where he stood on the river-bank. "Signor Farini, are you all right?"

Farini, as if emerging from a dream, shook his head and turned. "Yes, yes. Perfectly all right." He flashed a weak smile. "Shall we prepare for this little walk in the water?"

The blacksmith produced some hand-made stilts he'd fashioned for the big event, described on handbills appearing everywhere as "The Most Spectacular and Dangerous Stunt of Signor Farini's Amazing Career."

"They are metal stilts, sir, the strongest ever made," the blacksmith said proudly as he helped Farini mount the stilts and strapped them to his legs. "I guarantee you they'll withstand the power of the current."

"The stilts may withstand the pressure, but will I?" Farini replied. He tested the stilts, which elevated him about four feet off the ground, by walking in little circles. The stilts narrowed at the bottom to give him more traction on the riverbed.

Hundreds of spectators sitting on a slope of grass along the riverbank applauded Farini's stilt-walk. He waved in their direction. They were early birds in search of the best vantage point. They'd seen the handbills and they knew there'd be more dangerous stilt-walking to come.

He turned back to the blacksmith and nodded his head in approval. "They're very well made," he said, bringing a proud grin to the face of the smithy.

Farini had mastered stilt-walking as a youngster in Port Hope. One day in his teens he'd even won a 100-yard dash on stilts at the Port Hope Fall Fair.

He placed a hand on the blacksmith's shoulder and said with a straight face, "Do these stilts come with a money-back guarantee?"

"Oh, absolutely, sir," replied the blacksmith, missing completely the jest in Farini's question. "Or I'll replace them with a brand new pair." Only then did the smithy realize Farini was joshing. Where he was going with the stilts, if they snapped or bent, he'd not likely be coming back for another pair.

A huge cheer arose from the spectators, now numbering in the thousands, when Farini placed first his right stilt, then his left into the water rushing along the bank of the river. Using a long metal pike, Farini carefully probed the river bottom, seeking the best footing. He had decided to enter the river about 50 yards above the brink of the American Falls. His destination, about 100 yards away, was Goat Island.

Farini was almost overwhelmed when he felt the power of the current embracing the thin stilts supporting his legs. He moved into the rushing water slowly and cautiously. With each step he placed his pike and his stilts carefully on the river bottom, trying to avoid the slippery rocks just under the surface. He told himself to relax and let the tension seep from his powerful arms and shoulders. He estimated that the current, while strong, was not likely to sweep his false legs out from under him. Still, he must not underestimate its raw power. He must be alert for any surprises.

Above the roar of the water crashing over the Falls, he heard raucous voices from the shore, where a gang of beer-drinking youths had gathered.

"Hurry up, Farini. Get a move on."

"Get closer to the brink, Farini!"

"Yes, the brink. Move closer to the brink!"

What kind of fool do they think I am? thought Farini. He didn't dare move any closer to the brink. It was there the water seemed to leap up and become even more turbulent, as if trying to avoid the unavoidable—a long nosedive into the rock-strewn chasm below.

"The brink," they began to chant, "the brink! Get closer to the brink!"

That these drunken yokels were jeering his efforts angered him. He decided to give them a thrill they'd long remember. He held his right stilt firmly under his arm, raised a finger and pointed to the brink. The crowd roared its approval. Then he turned and moved with the current until he was only a few feet from the lip of the mighty cataract. In the history of the world, no man had stood where he now stood. The knowledge gave him a thrill, but he dared go no closer.

Peering along the lip of the Falls he became almost hypnotized as he witnessed the incredible weight of water relentlessly soaring over the brink. Suddenly he felt a strange temptation to release his stilts and embrace the current, to let it capture him and soar with it unafraid over the beckoning brink, shrieking with delight like a child on a water slide. The thought quickly vanished and he found himself gripping his pole even tighter.

In the few moments he'd been standing there, tons of green-blue-brown-white water had tumbled over the lip and vanished from his sight, only to be replaced by tons more and tons more after that. Within seconds the never-ending mass crashed furiously into the gigantic boulders below. From where he stood, the roar was deafening.

Slowly he turned his stilts and moved once again in the direction of the small island. It was still a long distance off. He was soaked to the skin by now and his body was becoming numb from the cold. *Hurry*, he told himself, *for you are losing feeling in your legs. If you hit a deep spot, your legs will drop below the waves and you may easily be swept over the Falls.*

In front of him, a tiny island, made up mostly of boulders, rose from the churning water. There was even a thin, scrubby tree rising from it. "Perhaps," he murmured, "I can rest there for a moment. It's only a few strides away."

He took a step, then another. Suddenly, he stumbled slightly and, in an effort to regain his balance, over-compensated. His right stilt slid between two rocks and became lodged there. Immediately, Farini knew he was in peril. He sank his pike in the water and tried to dislodge the rocks. No luck. Adjusting his weight, he yanked hard on the shaft of his pike, but it did not budge. It, too, was wedged between the rocks!

Gauging the distance to the small island, he decided he couldn't leap far enough to land on the rocks—even if he unstrapped his stilts. But...if he could somehow vault the distance, he just might be able to grasp hold of the overhanging branches of the small tree. Then he thought: *What if the roots of the tree are so shallow they pull right out when I grab them—if I'm able to grab them. I'll be swept over the Falls in a flash.*

But I have no other choice. I will have to risk it. He could feel his right stilt begin to buckle under the weight of his body and the force of the current. *I may have to ask that smithy for a new pair, after all!*

Spectators on shore began to realize that Farini was in deadly peril. Max, Marty and Trudy rushed toward the riverbank.

"Max, is there anything we can do?" Marty asked anxiously.

"Not a thing," Max replied grimly. "It's all up to the Signor now."

Trudy turned away and began to sob.

Farini, as he had so many times in the past, fought back panic. Slowly, he turned his body toward the island. With one hand, he loosened the leather straps holding his right stilt in place. He didn't dare unstrap the left. He took a deep breath, gathered his strength and, using his pike in the manner of a pole-vaulter, threw himself violently over the water to the cluster of rocks. Desperately, he reached out for the branches of the tree. "Got you!" he shouted as his left hand gripped a branch.

His lower body splashed into the water and he bellowed in pain as he landed on a submerged rock. It smashed into his side, bruising his ribs. He felt his legs scraping along some jagged rocks. There was a moment of terror when the small tree lurched and he felt the branch slipping through his grip. Leaves squirted through his fingers and sped off—gone instantly over the Falls.

Fighting back fear, he thought: *The tree will be next to go. The strain on its roots is too great.* The tree shifted again, sending his heart into his mouth. A pebble bounced up and struck him on the cheek. But the roots did not spring free. They clung tenaciously to the meagre soil. Inch by inch, gasping and shivering, more frightened than he'd ever been in his life, Farini managed to heave himself onto the island. He lay there shivering, face down among the wet, slippery rocks and a small patch of grass. His eyes were closed, his chest was heaving and a trickle of blood streamed down one cheek. He muttered a prayer, thanking God for sparing him from a horrible death.

"Now we can do something," Max cried. "Come on, let's go for help!"

Along the banks of the river, the spectators had been watching in grim but fascinated horror as

Farini fought for his life. They burst into wild applause when he reached the tiny island above the brink of the Falls. After a few minutes, however, when he failed to rise and take a bow, some of them began to jeer his failed performance. They verbally abused him.

"I lost a big wager on you today," bellowed a man in overalls. "I bet you wouldn't last ten seconds in that river. Getting to that dern island cost me a bundle."

Another man cupped his hands to his mouth and yelled, "Farini the Fake! Farini the Fool! I want my 25 cents back! Don't expect any of us to come out there to save you!"

A third man joined in. "Farini's conned us," he complained to the crowd. He cupped his hands and hollered at Farini, "No boat can rescue you and it'll soon be dark. See how you like sittin' on them rocks all night. Bet you never planned to go any farther than that rock in the first place."

"Right on," shouted the man in overalls. "After dark you can bet old Soper will come along, throw Farini a rope and drag him off that rock. Then the two of them will count all the money they made today. I say leave him there and forget about him. Let's go home."

It didn't help Farini's cause that Mr. Soper, having collected the admissions, was nowhere to be found and therefore could offer neither an explanation nor, more importantly, a refund.

The crowd was convinced Farini and Soper had fleeced them.

"They're frauds and swindlers!" shouted a young boy. His little brother took up the cry. "Yeah, frogs and squigglers!" he echoed, his mispronunciation drawing a laugh. The boy walked close to the riverbank and spit in the direction of Farini. "And to think you used to be my hero!" he shouted. He picked up a small stone at the water's edge and threw it at Farini. Other boys scrambled to the bank and began tossing stones, too. Their parents half-heartedly scolded them. Some of the adults looked angry enough to join them in the stone tossing.

Farini was in shock. Not only from the effects of his icy ordeal, but from shock over the sudden betrayal of his fans.

"I was their hero," he muttered to himself, unable to believe his eyes, his ears.

Had they *really* called him a swindler, a fool and a fraud? Had they really turned on him as Colcord had predicted? How will you deal with it, Colcord had said, when the adulation and the glory is all gone? "Now I know how Blondin feels," he said bitterly. "I didn't think it would ever happen to me."

It began to rain, and the spectators began to hurry away under raised umbrellas, gathering up soggy blankets and full picnic baskets as they fled. Farini groaned. Miserable, he watched forlornly until the last of them disappeared along the path that led into town.

He looked across the heaving water and blinked, not believing his eyes. His eyelids fluttered and his heart pounded with joy. There she was, standing under a tree, her head in her hands. Andrea. Shiny raindrops landed like diamonds in her golden hair. Tears mixed with raindrops ran down her pale face and she dabbed at her nose with a lace handkerchief.

Farini's eyes misted over and a lump rose in his throat. He raised one arm and waved, weakly. It was just about all he could manage.

She stared at him across the raging river for a long moment. She waved back, using just her fingers. But no smile brightened her face and her tears continued to flow.

Oh, Andrea, he found himself thinking. *Why didn't you stay on the carriage to Port Hope? What made you change your mind and come back—to what? To witness this failure, this disaster? And all because of my pride and my vanity. How insensitive I've been. I've never felt so distraught.*

Shivering, Farini rolled onto his back, sat up as best he could and dropped his head onto his chest. He closed his eyes and pressed his hands to his ears, trying to block out the roar of the river that surrounded him. He thought of Andrea, of his unborn child. He wondered why he had allowed his thirst for adventure, his lust for fame and fortune to pull him away from the things in life that really mattered.

Andrea was right, he realized. His fans didn't care about him. They didn't respect his courage, his daring and his skill. Most of them were hoping to see him fail and be crushed. He had a vision of them telling their friends and kinfolk, "I was there, right there, when that fool Farini went over the Falls and met a horrible death. But the man had it coming. He went too far. Imagine trying to cross above the mighty Falls on a flimsy pair of stilts. Can't be done. He was crazy, all right. But he gave us all one big thrill at the end, I'll say that for him."

Farini shook his head. He still didn't understand. Now that the fans who had come to see him fail had actually seen him stumble, miraculously avoiding sudden death, they were furious. They had taunted him and stoned him! Would they not be satisfied until he actually tumbled into the gorge to his death?

CHAPTER 18

MCSORLEY COMES THROUGH

Farini rose to one knee and cupped his hands, and through the pouring rain and the roar of water he shouted to Andrea. She had raised an umbrella and had rushed close to the riverbank. "Andrea, do you think you can find somebody to help me? Somebody with a good rope?"

"I'll go back to the hotel," she called back. "Surely somebody there will be willing to help. Hopefully, I'll be back before dark."

She hurried off down the path to her carriage. On the road back to town, Andrea and her driver came across the Mitchell brothers and Trudy hurrying along.

"Get in! Get in!" Andrea shouted. The carriage slowed and the three teenagers climbed aboard.

"Andrea!" Trudy shouted in surprise. "We thought you'd left. We're going for help."

"Well, I changed my mind. But you're right. We've got to get help for my husband. What do you suggest, Max?"

"The hotel is close by. Let's start there," he replied.

The horse and carriage bounced along the road and stopped at the hotel. Within the hotel there was a tavern—the Billy Goat. Andrea pushed her way through the swinging doors, ignoring a sign in the front window that read "Gentlemen Only! No One Under 21." The Mitchells and Trudy were close behind.

The raucous, earthy chatter from the crowded tavern slowly faded and ceased, and chair legs scraped the floor as patrons turned in frank astonishment to witness the long-skirted intruder and her three fresh-faced companions. Andrea stood there a moment, her dress wet with rain, her high button shoes coated with mud.

"Lady," hollered an outraged man with a stein of beer raised to his mouth, "you ain't s'pose to be in here. No females allowed." He stepped forward as if to block her path. "And no kids neither."

"Get out of my way!" snapped Andrea, poking the tip of her umbrella into the man's large belly. He staggered back, belched and sat down.

"I'm looking for a man!" Andrea shouted.

"Well, you come to the right place," wisecracked someone in the back of the room. The men burst out laughing.

Undaunted, Andrea stepped boldly into the room, frowning frostily at the man who'd shouted.

Like a scolded child, he sat down and muttered, "Sorry."

"Now then, I need a big man, a strong man. This is extremely urgent. My husband is in great peril and I mean to save him. But I need help."

"Sounds like you need McSorley," suggested a man in a plaid suit sitting at the bar. "He's the strongest man around."

"That's right, he is," someone else shouted from the middle of the room. "He's strong enough to throw me out of this place every time I get disorderly." The other men burst into laughter.

"And where's this McSorley?" Andrea asked.

"Right here, ma'am." A huge man with a freckled face and broad shoulders moved out of the shadows. He doffed a large hat and smiled. "What can I do for you?"

"My husband is Farini the ropewalker," she pleaded, "and he's trapped on a tiny island at the brink of the American Falls. If it continues to rain, the river will rise and he'll surely be swept over the Falls to his death."

"Then let's go, ma'am," he said, taking her firmly by the arm and steering her out of the tavern. Max, Marty and Trudy followed close behind. "These young people are friends of mine," Andrea explained.

"Good," he said. "We may need them. First we'll find us a long rope. Then we'll get your husband off that rock pile he's sitting on. By the way, ma'am, I've seen your husband perform. He's a dern fine man and brave as a lion."

They squeezed into the carriage and raced down the street to the livery stable. "Wait here!" said McSorley curtly. He hopped out and went inside. Two minutes later he emerged with an enormous coil of rope and the biggest pair of work gloves the boys had ever seen.

"Looks like bear paws," muttered Marty.

"Here, boys. Grab this gear!" he called out.

They raced the carriage to the brink of the Falls. It began to rain harder. Fog rolled in, thick as paint. It was growing dark. Andrea ran to the river's edge. "I can't see him anymore," she wailed. "Farini! Farini! Are you still out there?" Black water swirled around her ankles. If Max hadn't come up and grabbed her by the arm, she might easily have been swept away by the current.

"Yes, I'm still here, Andrea," Farini answered in a faint voice. "But the water seems to be rising. Go back to the hotel and rest. Think of the baby."

"Farini!" boomed McSorley. "Name's McSorley. I aim to pluck you off that rock. Got a long rope here. Can't throw it to you if I can't see you. You may have to spend the night out there. Can you wait until dawn?"

"Looks like I'll have to," came the answer. "But if it keeps on raining I may be up to my neck in water by morning."

Andrea had an idea. "Can't we light a big fire, Mr. McSorley? Would that give us enough light to see my husband?"

"It might," he agreed, "if it wasn't so foggy. Besides, all the firewood around here is soaking wet. No, we'll just have to wait for the first light of dawn."

Max had another idea. "Do we need more help, Mr. McSorley? Shall Marty and I run back to the tavern and get some of the men to come help us?"

McSorley said, "Naw. None of them men would be of any use. Most of 'em would need sobering up to be of help. Besides, I can do this on my own. You'll have to trust me."

McSorley urged Andrea to wait out the night in her room at the hotel. "Think of your delicate condition, ma'am," he said, blushing.

"No, no, I won't hear of it," she protested. She did make a hasty trip back to town to purchase some food. Then she returned to the riverbank to join McSorley, the Mitchell brothers and Trudy in an all-night vigil.

"I passed a small pavilion along the trail," she said. "We could wait there and stay dry. Farini would want us to."

For the next few hours they sat at a picnic table in the pavilion as the rain splattered the roof and fog crept in from the open sides. They shared cheese, crackers and a bottle of milk.

Just before dawn, it stopped raining. Slowly, the blackness of night surrendered to the pink flush of an eagerly awaited sunrise. The fog thinned and then vanished in the advancing light.

McSorley had fallen asleep. His huge head was bent to his chest, his hat had toppled off and the thunderous sound of his snoring reverberated throughout the pavilion.

"Mr. McSorley, wake up, please. It's time to go." Andrea tapped him on the arm several times.

"Huh," he blurted, grunting until he shook himself awake. "Yes, ma'am. Time to go. Indeed it is."

From the riverbank, they could see Farini huddled on the rocks. The rising river had submerged all but the largest. Farini clung to it, his legs in the current, buffeted by the waves.

"We don't have much time," Max said urgently. "The current is going to pull him off that rock."

"Please hurry, McSorley!" Andrea pleaded.

"You stay right here, ma'am," he instructed Andrea. "I'm going to move upstream a ways. I'll be heaving the rope into the current and hope it floats downstream close to your husband. Max, you come with me."

"Good mornin', sir," McSorley shouted to Farini. He told him, "Be ready to reach for the rope. It'll be moving fast."

McSorley and Max walked some distance upstream. McSorley handed one end of the rope to Max. "Loop one end around that big tree and tie it fast," he ordered. The big man took the rest of the coil and hurled it across the water. But it fell short and he pulled it in. "My arms are thick and strong but they're not much good at throwin' things," he complained.

"I'm a pitcher in baseball," Max said. "How about I try?"

"Sure, son. You may have the skill I lack. Go for it!"

Max's attempt was much more accurate. The rope sailed high in the air, splashed into the river and in seconds swept past Farini's rocky perch. Despite the numbness in his hands, Farini's fingers shot out and he came up clutching the rope.

"Great catch!" shouted McSorley. "Now tie the end around your waist and we'll reel you in."

Farini's shaking hands struggled to secure the rope around his waist. Finally he was able to knot it loosely in place. His fingers, chilled to the bone, tried to tighten the loop and failed. It would have to do.

He waved to McSorley. "Let's do it," he shouted.

McSorley donned his workman's gloves, drew the rope taut, and dug in his heels by the base of the tree. Max gripped the rope lower down. A nod of McSorley's large head told Farini he was ready.

Farini gripped the rope tightly with both hands and belly-flopped into the water. The force of the current slammed into him, taking his breath away and forcing him to his knees. The current whipped him away from the island. In an instant he was swept to the very brink of the Falls. If he plunged over, the rope would surely snap or be cut through by the sharp edge of rock that formed the brink.

He had an overwhelming desire to try to pull himself hand over hand along the rope. But he didn't dare release a hand, not even for a second, for he needed them both, plus all of his strength, just to hang on. If he released a hand, the river would surely pluck him from the rope, swallow him up and spit him over the falls.

The taut rope strained against his weight. He felt himself moving against the mighty current, and he realized McSorley, with Max's help, was doing his job, inching him away from the Falls and sudden death.

Through the waves that splashed into his face, stinging his skin, he could see McSorley, his muscles straining, his barrel chest heaving, his large head thrown back, the cords in his thick neck standing out, pulling tenaciously on the rope. The big man's brute strength gave him confidence. And Max was showing a lot of upper-body strength, too.

Then McSorley's feet slipped out from under him and the rope went slack momentarily. Farini let out a cry as he was swept back toward the brink. He saw Andrea, Marty and Trudy rush over to help McSorley.

They helped to pull the big man erect. Andrea and Trudy gripped McSorley by his belt and suspenders. Marty grabbed a section of rope. Together they pulled Farini away from the precipice and edged him closer to the riverbank. He took a breath and swallowed some water. He began to cough and choke. Suddenly, he felt a layer of rock under his feet, but his legs were too weak to stand on it, the current too powerful for him to gain a footing.

He was only inches from the riverbank and safety but his strength was ebbing. It was no use. He would have to give up. His hands were slipping on the rope; he'd swallowed water and was almost exhausted. The rope began to slip through his fingers—first an inch or two, then a foot. He would have to let it go, let the angry river and the waiting Falls claim him. He could hear Andrea screaming, "Hang on, darling! Hang on!" But he couldn't hang on. He heard himself shouting, "I love you Andrea. Forgive meeee..."

He began to lose consciousness. His body went slack, his frozen fingers and aching arms relaxed. He closed his eyes and let go of the rope.

At that instant, a mighty arm gripped him by the wrist. A sharp pain shot up his arm and revived him. He felt himself being yanked bodily from the current. He grunted as he was dragged roughly up a rocky embankment. Breathless and groggy, not quite sure what had happened, Farini opened his eyes and saw McSorley grinning down at him. Then McSorley was lifting him in his strong arms and carrying him to safety—to a patch of green grass and into the outstretched arms of Andrea.

McSorley was talking rapidly about his rescue. "I promised your lady I'd get you out," he said, "and I did. But man, it was close. When I saw you was just about done, and I saw the rope slippin' through your fingers, I told Max and Marty to hang on to the rope for dear life. Good thing those kids are strong. I ran like heck to where you were. Got there just in the nick of time, too. You were just close enough to the river's edge so I could reach out and grab you."

"Thank you, McSorley," Farini said. "Thank you, my friend."

For several minutes Farini lay with his head on Andrea's shoulder. He could feel her rapid heartbeat, her soft hands caressing his face. He heard her murmur, "I was so frightened I'd lost you and I'm so happy you're safe."

McSorley had wandered off for a few minutes, thoughtfully giving the couple some time to savour the joy of being reunited. His whistling announced his return and he emerged from the woods with some fresh bread and a container of milk under his arm.

"Compliments of Mr. Curtis, a farmer who lives not far from here, and his good wife," he explained, offering the food to Farini. "Curtis says he's a big fan of yours. Hopes to see you back on your rope again next season."

When Farini said he'd rested enough, Max and Marty pulled him to his feet. "You can eat and drink while we ride back into town," Andrea said, putting an arm around his waist. "We must get back to the hotel and get you into a hot tub. And have the doctor examine you for cracked or broken ribs. Come along Mr. McSorley, you'll need some nourishment too. And several hours sleep, I imagine."

"There's not enough room in the carriage for all of us," Max said. "Marty and Trudy and I will walk back. We'll see you later."

In the carriage, Farini said, "I'm overwhelmed at what you did, McSorley. You are a real hero. I thank you and I apologize for putting you to so much trouble." He reached out his hand and shook the much larger hand "And to you, Andrea," he said, placing an arm around her shoulder. "And to Max and Marty and Trudy. What a great team! I thank you all for saving my life."

"Your brave wife deserves most of the credit, Farini," said McSorley with a broad grin. "The way she stormed into the Billy Goat Tavern and asked for help. Now that was somethin' to see. Them other fellas just gawked at her but I felt it was a real honour to be able to give her a helping hand. I always knew you was a champion, Farini, but now I know your wife is one too. You're a lucky, lucky man. Without her, you wouldn't be headed back to town, chewing on fresh bread and pinchin' yourself to see if you're still alive."

They came to a clearing and the breathtaking beauty of the morning sunlight on the Falls caught their eye. Farini asked McSorley to bring the carriage to a halt. Without uttering a word, Farini slipped from the carriage and walked slowly to the edge of the cliff overlooking the gorge. For a long time his glistening eyes devoured the glorious panorama. Perhaps he was thinking of past triumphs: how he'd walked his rope across the chasm while thousands cheered; how he'd engaged in a spectacular duel with The Great Blondin; how he'd proved that a farm boy from Port Hope could be the daring Frenchman's equal—and then some.

No one, not even Andrea, ever knew what emotions he felt at that particular moment in his fascinating life. For he never talked of it. Never. She only sensed that it was a moment of great importance—to her husband and to their future together.

Somewhere a bird was singing. A leaf fell from a tree and brushed Farini's shoulder. He didn't notice. McSorley shifted his weight from foot to foot and began to look puzzled. Andrea cast worried glances at her husband's back as he continued to stare out over the Falls.

Slowly he turned and a brilliant smile lit up his face. He walked toward them and spoke directly to his wife. "It's over, Andrea," he said. "There'll be no more walking of ropes over the Falls. No more spectacular stunts. It's time to move on to other things in life, like learning to be a good husband and father." He took her small hand in his. "Let's go home, Andrea."

Andrea cried out in joy. Then she hugged him and kissed him. Finally she said, "Does this mean we've seen the last of Niagara Falls, dear?"

"Oh, no," Farini said. "We'll come back someday soon—and have a real honeymoon."

CHAPTER 19

END OF THE DREAM

In a small longhouse on the reserve of Tumbling Waters, three young people stirred in their sleep, opened their eyes and rose from their mats—all at the same time. It took them a moment to realize where they were. Then they began to laugh and chatter.

"It was a fabulous dream," Trudy said. "It was so real—for me at least."

"It was for us, too," said Max, a big grin on his face. "When the Little People put you in a dream, they make it really convincing, don't they? And how it's possible for three people to share the same dream is beyond me."

Marty shrugged. "I don't care how the Little People do it, I'm just glad they do it. And that they allow us to be a part of it."

Trudy smiled. "I loved going down the River of Time to Niagara Falls and meeting Farini and his wife," she said. "There's never been a performer like him. His stunts on the rope were breathtaking."

Marty clasped his hands together and looked up. "Thank you, McSorley, wherever you are. Thank you for rescuing Farini when it looked like he was a goner. You're a mighty strong man, McSorley." Marty turned to Max and Trudy and held up his thumb and index finger. "Farini was that close to going over the Falls and into the rocks below. He went further into that river than any man will ever go."

"*Farther*, Marty. He went farther, not further. You say farther when you talk about distance."

"Okay, wise guy, farther. Anyway, *further* to what I was saying, what a surprise when Andrea showed up at the last minute!" Marty said. "I liked her. She was a nice lady."

"And she loved Farini," said Trudy. "It wasn't easy for her, being married to a man who risked his life almost every day."

Just then the door to the longhouse opened and Chief Echo walked in. He had a thick book under his arm. "Good, you're awake," he said. "The Little People said you would be. How are you feeling?"

"Wonderful," Trudy answered. "Thank you, Chief, for allowing me to paddle down the River of Time with Max and Marty. It was a journey I'll never forget."

"I'm glad you enjoyed it," said the Chief, "I'm quite sure you found it entertaining and educational. Let's sit down. My wife Esmerelda is bringing us tea."

He tapped the book under his arm with a finger and held it up. "It's called *Daredevils of Niagara*," he said. "I thought you might have some questions."

"I do," Marty said, eager to be first. "Did other ropewalkers cross the gorge after Farini? And did any of them fall off the rope and drown?"

Chief Echo said, "Good question, Marty. Several other ropewalkers crossed the gorge. But none of them performed the spectacular stunts that Farini and Blondin did. It may surprise you, but none of the walkers ever fell into the gorge. Not one. Despite that perfect record, ropewalkers are now banned from crossing over the Falls. That era is part of our history now. Most people have forgotten about Blondin and Farini."

"Gee, that's too bad," Marty said. "Those two fellows had tremendous courage."

"So did Colcord and McMullen," Max added. "There aren't many men who would trust a ropewalker to carry them piggyback over the gorge."

"I'll bet they're the only two people in history to do it," Marty piped up. "Right, Chief?"

Chief Echo nodded.

"We might have done it," Marty boasted. "Max

said he would. And I would have too, but only if there'd been a parachute handy."

"When did people start going over Niagara Falls in a barrel?" Max asked.

Chief Echo had to look it up. "Says here the first person to go over the Falls in a barrel was a woman—Annie Taylor—in 1901. She survived. She was 61 years old but she claimed to be 40."

"Ten years later—in 1911—Bobbie Leach became the first man to go over the Falls in a barrel. He survived too. Can you believe he died a few years later when he slipped on an orange peel?"

"What happened to Farini after he left Niagara Falls?" Max asked the Chief.

"According to this book," said the Chief, "Farini led a happy and productive life. It was marred by one great tragedy. A year after his stunning achievements at Niagara Falls, he performed on his rope in Cuba. It was there he carried his wife on his back across a bullring. As he neared the end of the rope, she leaned back to wave to the spectators and lost her balance, tumbling to her death into the seats far below.

"Oh, no!" cried Trudy.

"Farini was devastated but he did not retire and fade into obscurity. He went on to become creator of the Flying Farinis, an act hugely popular in Europe. He, of course, was the star performer.

"Farini was also an inventor, credited with introducing the safety net to circus acts and the folding seats to theatres. Some credit him with inventing the parachute. Less successful was a strange boat he invented shaped like a cylinder, which sank on its maiden voyage into the waters of Lake Ontario.

"During the American Civil War, he assisted the North with inventions like special boots designed for walking on water and rope bridges. In 1885 he embarked on a dangerous eight-month expedition through the Kalahari Desert in South Africa. There he claimed to have discovered some evidence of a lost civilization. In the latter stages of his life he became an accomplished horticulturist, writer and painter. He returned to Port Hope where he died in January 1929, a victim of a flu epidemic.

"He was an amazing man," Max said quietly.

There was a knock on the door of the longhouse.

"That will be Esmerelda," the old Chief said. "It's time for some tea."

THE REST OF THE STORY

While the fascinating story of Willie Hunt—The Great Farini—is based on fact, the author has taken some liberties with these facts for the purpose of entertaining young readers. Farini's incredible feats at Niagara Falls are a matter of record and have been well chronicled. Since little is known of Farini's first wife (he was married four times), his romance and marriage to Andrea were fictional, as were the roles played by Jimmy Jenkins, McSorley and others. However, Colcord and McMullen (his real name may have been Mullen) were real men of great courage—the only men in history to be carried piggyback across the Niagara gorge.

Your author may have understated many of Farini's amazing talents and accomplishments. And Blondin's as well. For example, Blondin once pushed a wheelbarrow across his rope while walking blindfolded. He once crossed over the gorge with his feet inserted in peach baskets. He hung from his rope by his feet. He did somersaults and headstands on the rope. Later in his career, performing in England, he was severely criticized for strapping his five-year-old daughter into a wheelbarrow and taking her for a ride along his rope—a stunt that so angered onlookers it almost ended his career.

Farini, irked at criticism from spectators that he walked too slowly on one of his rope walks, almost trotted across it on one occasion, setting a record time for such a long traverse. There were occasions when Farini hung from the rope with both hands, then one hand, then by his feet—and finally by one foot. And no man ever tried to duplicate his walk while completely covered by a sack. Nor did anyone else attempt to match his death-defying feat of stilt-walking through the turbulent waters above the brink of the American Falls.

Farini's near-tragic stilt-walk across the cascading Niagara River—while true—took place some time later than described. Some historians claim that incredible stunt was just a practice run, that a much larger crowd had planned to see him attempt the superhuman feat one week later. One version of the rescue attempt has him tying the rope thrown to him to a tree on the island on which he was stranded. The other end was attached to a tree on shore and he saved himself by walking the rope to safety.

While he never again returned to Niagara Falls after that daring walk in the water, he did not give up his passion for ropewalking—not always with the approval of the crowd. Late in his career, he too heard the critics roar angrily when he took a four-year-old girl, strapped into a wheelbarrow, across a rope in Buffalo, New York. During several practice runs his young passenger laughed and appeared to be enjoying the experience. But when a huge crowd gathered to watch the real event, the lass became alarmed and burst into tears during the walk. The crowd below howled at Farini and threatened him with bodily harm if he didn't get her down immediately—not an easy task when one is 100 feet above the ground and halfway across a taut rope.

Farini's second wife was a wealthy lady from Nova Scotia, but little is known of this relationship. In 1871 he wed Alice Carpenter, an Englishwoman who bore him two sons. The union ended in a messy divorce in 1878. His fourth wife was Anna Muller, a German socialite and concert pianist 15 years his junior.

I urge all of my young readers to refrain from walking on ropes or wires at any time and at any height. It is extremely dangerous, falls are common and they often result in serious injury to the unskilled beginner.